Perfect

The Perfect Mask

Acknowledgements

I want to thank my best friend Heather Hynd for allowing me to use her experiences and character in this book; highlighting issues that she has struggled with from being a mum to a child with special needs and all that brings with it, knowing she is one of many who have learned and still learning ways to cope and understand the vast challenges that autism brings. Also, her comedic ways, and her brilliant boys Jack and Liam who bring fun and love to my life.

I'd like to thank my good friend Leonie Darby Howes for agreeing to be the model for the front cover of this book, being brave enough to show an example of her taking off her mask as she also understands the pressures of raising children with the added demands of having a child with additional needs, trying to balance life, while raising her amazing girls Lydia and Poppy.

I'd like to thank my family for always being supportive and listening to me, helping me in so many different ways to be the mum I need to be.

Derek Cross who designed my front cover beautifully and patiently when I couldn't make up my mind, and last but not least, my children, my reason for getting up in the morning and the cause of tears, laughter, frustration, big love and the biggest learning curve I have ever found myself on. They are amazing, truly unique and I'm lucky to say they are mine. Alex and Ash.

Introduction

Perfect. What a word. What does it even mean? Is it what you think others perceive it to be as you continue to put on a show of 'perfection.' Hiding behind the mask you created. Why is it not enough to be as you feel, each and every day?

There is too much information about being a mother and often not enough. Information overload on how you 'Should' do things, what is 'Expected'. It's too easy to pick apart someone for their failings and not just privately anymore as we have this amazing thing called social media just waiting to criticize our every move; yet we display it tentatively, in the hope that it somehow passes the invisible test of standards someone put there for us, watching everybody else's lives through that same screen, wondering if their snap shot of perfect really is as it seems; or if like you, there are cracks in that smile, dark circles under the carefully applied make up and harsh words said between the loving couple holding their new baby resting their heads against each other's, waiting for the camera to click before walking in separate directions.

It's like an expectation and fluidly changes on each person's perception, depending on the mental state they are in that day. Reflecting back on a 'perfect' day with the kids while luxuriating in the bath, a cool glass of wine ready to sip and the kids already fast asleep is quite different to the vision of 'perfect' we may try to create to the outside world as we slip into our uniforms of what is socially acceptable and choose the mask we need for the day. Now I'm not talking about the hygiene masks we have been needing and using since the coronavirus outbreak. I mean the shields we put on, our make-up (I used to call it my battle armour. Only in my head though), the smile we show the world to make sure they know we are OK, the properly ironed clothes (That we really didn't have time to do, but we have to reflect a certain image don't we), the busy chatter of how productive we have been that morning already, the light voice that belies the empty feeling inside and the energy that denies how tired we really are. There are so many ways to wear a mask... the beautifully clean and tidy house, so organised so...perfect. Perfect to who? The visitor holding a coffee, chatting to her friend from work about her day, never really divulging her true feelings. That she actually wanted to be in sweatshirt and jogging bottoms with baggy knickers and no make-up, sprawled ALONE on her sofa watching tv that makes your mind melt because she has enough in her own brain to cope with anymore. But she smiles, she sits and makes pleasant conversation ending with we must do it again sometime and she enjoyed it, she *did* really. It's always nice to see friends, but real friends are the ones where your mask falls ever so slightly and they see that, but instead of helping you readjust it... They will not only empathise, but they will also let theirs slip too. Over time, you both don't need them with each other at all and can be free of the mask without judgement. That's real friendship in my view and I am so lucky to have it.

I have written this book for the women with masks.

CHAPTER ONE

Louise checked her list for the hundredth time, crossing off the last line:

~~Change litter tray~~

There was still lots more to do...

Wash up

Feed cats

Empty bin

Close curtains

Switch on downstairs lamp

Pack car.

Louise worked through the list with a practiced lightning speed, keeping an eye on the time. She wanted to be in the car and setting off before 8.30 so they could get there at a reasonable time and make the most of their first day.

The kids were engrossed in the TV, finishing off their breakfast. Louise decided to pack the car now so they wouldn't get under her feet.

Lucy was 6 and Amy 5, and at the age where you had to watch them both like a hawk, but Louise didn't have a drive and her car was parked round the corner... This required speed. Without announcing her departure, Louise grabbed the suitcase along with 4 bags, one on her back and three in the other hand and ran to the car. She would have packed it last night but was worried all their stuff would get stolen. No this was better. Dropping the keys twice, Louise finally managed to get the boot open, expertly throwing in the huge blue suitcase with all three of their clothes for the week, then dumping the other 4 bags on top, making room for Lucy's special buggy next to the suitcase she closed the boot and headed back indoors; breathing a sigh of relief seeing both the girls faces still eating their breakfast and staring at the screen as she wordlessly grabbed the other bags she had left by the front door; some of food, some toys, a bag just for the beach with their towels, sunscreen, hats, bucket and spade so she could grab that bag as soon as they arrived and go to the beach. Another bag for activities just for the car, first aid kit, handbag. Another rush to the car arranging where the bags needed to be. No, the first aid kit couldn't be in reach of the girls with all the medicines, that had to be in the front. Handbag in the front, toys where the girls could reach, snacks for the road...

"Mum."

Louise spun round to see Amy walking out into the road.

"Amy! Come on darling back inside, you don't have any shoes on."

"Where were you?" Amy's round beautifully chubby face stared expectantly at her, her soft brown curly hair falling in tendrils about her face, she shook them away looking worried.

"I was just here packing the car for our holiday!" Louise kept her voice light and cheery and was suddenly panicky about Lucy being left alone indoors.

"Come on, I'll race you back!"

Amy won of course, laughing as they hurried through the front door. Louise's heart beating a little faster when she couldn't see Lucy straight away.

"Lucy!" She called "Where are you?"

Louise's eyes scanned the living room, quickly dismissing the idea of upstairs, she hadn't been gone long enough for Lucy to climb upstairs, that would have taken her a while... The kitchen.

"Oh, let's put those back darling. We don't need those do we." Louise's hand closed over Lucy's as she was pulling the scissors out of the knife and fork drawer, Louise had left the baby gate open by mistake.

"Ok! So, you girls have finished your breakfast yeah? Well let's get shoes on and get going, shall we?" Louise kept upbeat despite the headache forming and thudding across her temples, keeping at bay the anxiety of the drive ahead and trying not to think of what could have happened with the scissors if she hadn't walked in when she did. She had been up since 6 that morning to try and be as organised as she was and still, they weren't ready to go.

Amy had her shoes on by now, pulling on her favourite see through jelly ones, she looked so pretty in her purple flower dress. Her curly hair in a loose ponytail, it was so long it was halfway down her back, beautiful but hard work with the knots her curls created. Lucy's hair was a lighter shade of brown and completely straight, she had a more angular look like Louise did, lovely

10

innocent eyes and slim build, she was wearing her yellow dress with white leggings. Lucy would always throw her legs up in the air, so leggings with a dress was a must for Lucy. They both looked lovely, and Louise felt a rush of affection for them, she tried hard not to get stressed as she thought of the things she still hadn't done and focused instead on helping Lucy with her shoes. When Lucy was safely strapped into her buggy, Louise ran around ticking off the last items on the list before grabbing every imaginable coat or jacket they may or may not need in the week ahead.

Ten minutes later, everyone in the car, house all locked up and the sat nav programmed in for Clacton, Louise was ready. She looked up at the rear-view mirror, smiling at the girls. She loved taking them on holiday, but this part was a real mission, and they hadn't even left the carpark.

Amy was opening her mouth wide over and over again as if to stretch out a feeling and Louise could see there was a definite stye coming in her left eye. Oh well the sea air would sort that right out... Hopefully.

"Amy why are you doing that with your mouth?"

"I don't know. My throat feels fuzzy, and this just feels good."

Oh no, not another infection please. Louise groaned inwardly while she mentally checked where she had packed the Calpol.

A quick glance at Lucy and she was humming loudly to herself, playing on the iPad. As Louise pulled away, she could feel her own eyes becoming scratchy and blurred. Ok, they were going to need some drops. They just had to get there first.

"Oh no, almost forgot!" Louise had noticed the other note she had left for herself on the dashboard.

Keys and money to Emma.

Emma fed the cats, Louise just had to drop the keys off to her before they went and try not to get into a long conversation so they could get on their way, was hard though; she was friends with Emma, and she always had interesting things to say and funny stories to tell through her animal boarding. They never had half enough time to catch up for proper chats, generally only meeting when one of them was in a rush.

Instead of knocking, Louise quietly popped the keys through the door and hurried back to the car.

"NOW we are on our way." Louise grinned at her gorgeous girls in the back.

"Shall we go on holiday girls?"

"Yes!" they both shouted at the same time.

Fighting down the anxiety of the hour and a half drive to Clacton on unfamiliar roads, Louise began to sing "We're all going on a summer holiday... No more worries for a week or two! Fun and laughter on our summer holidays, we'll make your dreams come......"

BEEEEEEP!! The car on the opposite side of the road was overtaking and came head on in front of Louise. Slamming on her brakes as hard as she could, bags sliding off their seats, girls rocked back in their chairs after the jolt of the seatbelt. She looked up in total shock to see not an apologetic face now passing on her right but a red, angry, bald man shouting profanities after what was clearly his fault as his wife slunk down in the seat next to him out of sheer embarrassment.

"FUCKING PRICK!" Louise's anger took over as she fought the urge to get out of the car.

"Mummy!" Amy brought her back to earth and instead she drove on hands still trembling with the shock of their near miss.

"I'm sorry. Sorry. That was naughty. Are you girls Ok?" A quick look in the mirror reassured Louise they were. "Anyway, where were we? We're all going on a summer holiday..."

CHAPTER TWO

The drive to Clacton was a lot calmer than the start and by the time they arrived, the summer sun was heating up nicely. Seagulls flew overhead filling the air with their calls, the salty breeze promised the long-awaited beach not too far away and Louise felt happy knowing she had got them there safely (just about.) It was time to find a parking space along the crowded streets; too early to check in at their caravan but they could still enjoy a few hours on the beach first.

Louise's eyes scanned around quickly for any spaces she could squeeze her beloved Hyundai Matrix into. It was an odd shaped car but Louise liked it, everything fit nicely, and she had plenty of boot space for everything they needed plus Lucy's special Maclaren buggy. She slowed as she saw a space right near a park, there were benches overlooking the beach on a hill. This was a good spot. Louise tried to zone out from Amy's excited chatter about the beach to be able to concentrate on not hitting any other cars.

"Just let me concentrate Amy please, talk to me in a minute."

"OK" Her cheery voice satisfied because they were actually there now, sitting back in her chair smiling, then her brow furrowed.

"Mummy-"

"Hang on sweetheart please."

"Mummy my throat hurts."

"Oh, does it?" Louise stole a glance in the mirror, Amy was holding her throat now. Damn it! She got tonsillitis every year, why now?!

"Ok, after I've parked, I will find the special medicine to make it all better OK?"

"OK."

Crunch. Louise hadn't been paying attention, not realising how close the car had been to the curb, scraping the underside of the car against it.

"Shit." She muttered under her breath; Amy had started to cry.

"Ok let's find that Calpol darling shall we, it will make you feel better in no time." Louise hopped out of the car, opened the boot and found what she was looking for straight away, Calpol in the first aid bag.

"Come on darling, have this medicine it will help."

"I don't want it, my throat hurts." Amy cried.

Louise counted to ten in her head.

"This will help, take the medicine and it will stop hurting."

Twenty minutes later and a lot of tears, all three of them were finally on their way to the beach. Lucy in her buggy, excited, she was flapping her hands and laughing and Amy skipping ahead in front pointing out the butterflies all around her. Louise bagged down with the picnic bag, blanket and buckets and spades was sweating now, and breathless by the time they got there. There was a steep hill to go down, Louise had to lean back while holding Lucy's buggy tight with all the bags balanced on her arms. It was a real mission, and she didn't get to fully appreciate the beautiful beach view as they approached. But they got there at last. Flat surface phew!

The beach was still fairly quiet, usually it got much busier at lunchtime and onwards but now it was nice. Louise walked for a few minutes until she saw a spot that seemed just right; toilets weren't too far away, café behind her and she could lift Lucy's buggy right on to the sand from here. Louise checked her phone. Nothing yet. Amy had run off towards the water.

"Amy! Stay where I can see you!"

"Hello babe!"

There she was Hayley Bale, 35 years old, same age as Louise. Wearing long denim shorts and a bright yellow vest top. Her wild dark brown, curly hair had escaped the constraints of her hairband, blue eyes sparkling with excitement, a huge grin on her face, looking happy and excited with her two boys Sam and Flynn. Louise's best friend.

"Oh, am I glad to see you!" Louise threw her arms round Hayley, *NOW* it was time to start their holiday.

Hayley was like a breath of fresh air for Louise, she was so upbeat and brought out the best in her. They had fun...always. Were able to laugh at situations they would otherwise find themselves stressed in and talk. Really talk.

They had been friends for four years now, had met at a local support group, not really connected there but met again at a hospital for appointments for Lucy and Flynn, talking while they waited (There wasn't much else to do in those dreary places) and Hayley was chatty, where Louise was more held back. But Hayley seemed to bring the conversation out in her and soon they were chatting away so in depth, a connection happened between them that Louise knew instinctively was something rare, and it was almost a shame when Lucy's name was called to see the doctor. After that they would meet up regularly with the kids on a Saturday for a play date. It wasn't easy being a single mum and they both had that in common, the children were of similar ages and Lucy and Flynn had very similar difficulties. This made their friendship quite unique, they understood each other when they found others didn't; shared the same frustrations about things that even their family struggled to understand, was regularly on the phone and had begun yearly holidays three years ago to make it easier, more enjoyable and less stressful.

"Come on Sam." Hayley helped Sam hop down on to the warm sand and watched as he ran over towards Amy.

"Hey Lucy, look who it is!" Louise pulled Lucy's buggy round so she could see Flynn while Hayley organised her bags on the sand.

Lucy reached out for Flynn to hold his hand and he let her for a little while but didn't like to be touched for too long so let go and sat looking at her instead. Neither of them wanted to get on to the sand just yet and Flynn hated the texture of it, Lucy needed a bit more time, so Hayley stayed with them while Louise had a walk towards the seashore to see the other two. She helped them pick shells, dig out a hole for the water to fill up and looked for crabs but all they found were dead ones. After an hour they swapped, Louise sat with Lucy and Flynn and Hayley ran round with Sam and Amy, kicking a ball about and splashing them with the waves as they came in.

It was like that with them two, they naturally took turns so that they could stretch their legs with the younger two and then sit with the older two. Lucy by now was happy to sit on the sand and Flynn wanted the waves so the juggle began; Hayley would have to take Flynn to the waves and lifted him up as they came in, he laughed and laughed as he got splashed time after time, making Hayley's face light up with happiness now he was finally enjoying himself, but she had to watch Sam by the waves too now as Flynn was on his feet and Louise had trouble seeing Amy by the sea as the beach had begun to fill up with people so had to move closer with Lucy who didn't really want to go but they made a game of chase the waves and soon she was laughing too.

By lunchtime everyone was happy to sit on the blanket and have something to eat. Lucy only wanted her crisps so every mouthful of sandwich was a bargain with the promise of crisps after and as soon as they had all had a reasonable amount of food, Hayley passed her friend a can of pink gin with a wink.

"Ooh now you're talking." Louise and Hayley chinked cans, leaning back against the wall while all four kids sat happily; Amy, Lucy and Sam were on the sand whilst Flynn sat on the blanket.

"What's the time?" Hayley asked.

"About half two now, after these we can have a slow get packed up and head to the site, our caravan keys should be ready by then eh."

"Sounds like a plan." Hayley tilted her head to the sun "It's been a good day so far hasn't it."

"And it's not over yet, we can get kids all settled for some dinner, then if we've got the energy take them to the park for half an hour."

"OK. Don't you want to take Lucy to the club house?"

Louise usually took Lucy to the clubhouse for some dancing, she loved the music, and the shows and Amy didn't like it at all. It wasn't the boys cup of tea either and Hayley liked to be settled with them by a certain time; another reason this worked so well between them, they supported each other to do all the activities even if some of the kids didn't like it.

"Well, I'm hoping I will get away with it tonight, I'm shattered to be honest and just want to chill out, I will take her tomorrow though if she wants to go."

"Oh, she will, she loves the music eh babe."

"Yeah, she does, she really rocks it once she is there."

Lucy LOVED music and the louder the better, she loved to feel it as well as hear it and she would dance until her legs gave way. Her mind was not as limited as her body, her body stopped her from doing what she desperately wanted and that was to be centre stage, singing and dancing for an audience. When Louise took her to the club house, Lucy would sit so patiently with the other children watching the show and the music would start afterwards. Louise would let

Lucy dance for a while, then she would get tired, her legs refusing to do the work Lucy longed them to do and so she would sit on the floor feeling the beat of the music through her body and Louise would then lift her up to dance for as long as she could hold her. They would leave then. Lucy very tired and falling asleep in the buggy as they walked back to the caravan.

"We've got all the unpacking to do as well haven't we" Louise said thinking about all the toys in the car, the colouring in and all the food, the suitcase. She groaned and drained the last of the pink gin.

"Shouldn't take us too long though, we're quick and can put some jacket potatoes in the oven while we're doing it."

"Good thinking, nice easy meal."

Hayley started packing up her bags and rolling up her blanket while the boys were occupied and Louise did the same, all their belongings ready on the path, just to get the kids shoes on and off they went. Sounds simple but in reality it took much longer and was a little stressful as Amy trod on a sharp stone, her Calpol was wearing off so her throat began to hurt again and so came her cries as Louise was trying to get Lucy's shoes on but she kept kicking them off until Louise decided Lucy didn't really need the shoes now anyway and got her settled in the buggy; while Hayley was struggling to get Flynn off the blanket because he was completely comfortable by now and didn't want to leave, Sam had built a sand castle and was scared to leave it in case it disappeared so Hayley took a photo of him standing next to it so it would last forever. Now Amy was really crying, and Louise felt the heat in her face as she tried to stay calm.

"Ok darling, the medicine is in the car, we just have to go up that hill."

Up that hill, that steep hill with all the bags and the picnic blanket.

"Come on let's go."

"Right behind you babe." Hayley now had Flynn in his buggy, and they were ready to go, side by side they started the climb up the hill. It was a hill they knew well, but the kids were getting heavier. As they pushed the buggies Louise and Hayley glanced at each other smiling, then immediately started racing. They ran all the way up and Louise really didn't know how she managed it, but they were laughing now, the stress gone.

"I beat you!" Hayley declared "Ha!"

"You had a head start!"

"No way!" Hayley laughed, "You never could handle me winning, could you?"

"I don't know what you're talking about. I think that may have been the first time you have ever won." Louise grinned.

"You *KNOW* I won that time."

Louise and Hayley laughed at the memory. When the kids were much younger; Amy 14 months and Lucy 2 and three months, Sam 6 months and Flynn a year and a half, both had double buggies and were heading back after a morning out with them feeding the ducks (Louise learned that Hayley actually had a fear of ducks, finding great pleasure in throwing the bread near her friends feet, doubled up in laughter as she shrieked dramatically, when they came waddling over to eat it), they had, had so much fun together. They kids threw the bread for the ducks near the lake but where they were so young, it was more for Louise and Hayley to be able to get fresh air and talk as they walked around.

"Time to head back mate, kids are getting restless" Hayley had said.

The sun was getting hot now too, it was the height of summer. The sticky heat beginning to make the girls uncomfortable in their buggies.

"Ok I make you right, let's head back up the hill."

Now the hill was so steep it was made to zig zag downwards because it would probably have been impossible to go straight up. A child's adventure on a bike and a parent's nightmare watching their child on the bike.

The two got ready at the bottom for their climb as they began to push the buggies. After an hour and a half of pushing the buggies around the lakes, picking the kids up to show them the ducks, stroke the passing dog and getting stuck in some mud, they were already tired. But they started upwards and as they passed the first zig zag (Not speaking to each other because it was impossible! You needed your breath!) Hayley passed Louise with a smile and raised her eyebrows, Louise understanding the unsaid challenge, pushed faster, going past Hayley and throwing her own smug look back at her, as she saw Hayley approaching quickly to her right, they both broke into a run at the same time. They ran until they got to the top, slowed down by their own laughter. Louise could not walk or speak for several minutes, her whole body exhausted, but she laughed! She Hadn't laughed like that for a long time.

"I won!" Hayley declared.

"No, you didn't!" When Louise got her breath back.

"I totally won! I passed you on that bend and got here first." Hayley grinned, knowing she was right.

"Mine are way heavier than yours so technically I won."

"Oh, here we go, here come the excuses."

They made fun of each other all the way back to their cars parked in a carpark round the corner.

"It's been great babe, as always." Hayley hugged her friend and waved goodbye to the girls.

"It has, have a great afternoon mate. Bye boys!"

"Oh, we will, we're on a high now, see you next Saturday, we'll do soft play yeah? Then maybe McDonald's."

"Ok great."

The two friends had gone their separate ways, smiling having shared their morning together.

It was lonely sometimes being a single parent. They both understood that. Especially with Lucy and Flynn's extra needs, they didn't feel that they fit in at certain places, so Louise just didn't go, and Hayley ended up walking out of one baby group once when someone had made a really insensitive comment. She held her usually quick tongue and left, feeling protective over her baby boy, she wanted him around people who accepted him for the way he was, and she had never forgotten that feeling that woman gave her when she made Hayley feel Flynn wasn't important.

They couldn't go home and rant at their partner as there wasn't a partner at home. It felt hard to explain their feelings of isolation to family because they always told them what an amazing job they were doing and how proud of them they were; It would almost be failing to admit the truth. That they felt lost, alone and scared of the future. In fact, the future seemed very overwhelming to even begin thinking about it, so instead of dwelling on it they would reach for the wine glass at 6.30 pm when kids were tucked up in bed knowing that would help them sleep, and not be kept awake by the 'what if's'.

Louise and Hayley connected, they got each other and became thick friends, bound together by a mutual understanding of their unique situation. Both Lucy and Flynn were born with cerebral palsy which meant a lot of things for both of them but at varying degrees, they were raising them alone and with Amy and Sam already overtaking their older siblings in strides. There was 14 months between Lucy and Amy and 14 months between Flynn and Sam, but Louise's girls were that much older. It was unusual their situation was so similar and although both Louise and Hayley were so different in many ways, they were the same in others and balanced each other out. Hayley was excitable and fun, always ready to join in a game, she wore her heart on her sleeve and gave generously to those she cared about.

Louise was more reserved, more careful with her words and fairly level-headed, she wouldn't always show what she was feeling, but once she made a friend, she too was generous and would help wherever she could. With Hayley she could be herself, she didn't have to pretend.

Back at the caravan now, Amy had taken some more Calpol so wasn't crying anymore; they both took turns sitting with the kids while the other got the suitcases out of the car and unloaded. Louise tried to find a number for the on-site doctor while she stayed inside.

"Oh great, found it." Sighing with relief knowing Amy would need antibiotics again.

"Ring 'em now babe, you may even get to see someone today." Hayley suggested as she heaved the heavy suitcase through the caravan door.

"Right OK, I'll do that." Louise dialled the number, getting through to a receptionist within a few rings.

"Hello, I was wondering if my daughter could see the doctor please?"

Louise got an appointment for an hour's time.

"I'll watch Lucy, you go with Amy and I'll stick some jacket potatoes in the oven, nice easy dinner for everybody."

"Oh, thanks mate, we'll be as quick as we can, will take the car in case I have to get antibiotics from the chemist in town."

Louise quickly threw all their luggage in their room; they were all sleeping in the double room. It was easier that way, then she didn't have to worry about Lucy getting up and wandering around in the night and Amy always felt safer too. She had time to explain to Lucy what was happening and that she was staying with Hayley. Lucy kept signing music, Louise knew she wanted to go to the clubhouse tonight, she absolutely loved it and guilt pulled at her insides when she tried to think of ways to say no because she was too tired.

"I don't know if it's on tonight."

Lucy looked down, disappointed.

"Ok, we will go OK. It's probably on. We will go after dinner."

Lucy's face lit up, her smile making Louise's heart melt. She kissed her forehead.

"See you soon."

Louise took Amy in the car to see the on-site doctor, they had never had to do this before, it was a little building outside of the swimming pool area. Louise knocked softly, unsure if this was the place.

"Come in." A jolly voice called from inside.

Louise and Amy walked through to find a small waiting area and a blonde woman sitting behind a desk looking up at them expectantly.

"How can I help you?" She smiled professionally as she waited.

"I'm here for my daughter Amy Barker. We have an appointment at 4.30 with the doctor."

"Ah yes, that's right. Please take a seat."

There wasn't anybody else in the waiting room for which Louise was thankful, hopefully they wouldn't wait too long. She had barely finished her thought when footsteps echoed down the small corridor.

"Amy Barker?" A middle-aged Indian doctor waited for them to get up, she smiled kindly at Amy. "Follow me please."

They followed the doctor to her room where she examined Amy's throat. Amy kept giggling when she shone the torch in her throat so she could peer in. "Say Aaahhhh" for me, nice and big."

"It hurts." Amy complained.

"Yes, it is infected, looks sore." The doctor concluded. "I will give a course of antibiotics for five days. You should make an appointment to see your regular doctor when you get home." The doctor smiled at Amy "This is for being a big girl." She found a lolly on her desk and gave it to Amy "Enjoy your holiday."

"Thank you, Doctor." Louise was grateful, and so pleased they were getting medicine early on, she should be feeling better in a day or so... hopefully.

Louise and Amy got back to the caravan half an hour later after picking up the antibiotics and waiting in line listening to some woman complain about her lack of medicines and the prescription being wrong.

"I'll unpack in the morning, I'm too tired now." Louise switched on the kettle to make a strong coffee "This will sort me out."

"Come on Amy you need to take your medicine now."

"I can take Lucy to the club house for an hour for you mate, I don't mind. You look tired."

"Oh, thanks Hayley, really. But no. I will take her. After dinner I'll have my second wind. And you can pour me a very large glass of wine for when I get back."

"Deal."

Lucy enjoyed every minute, she sat tall and expectantly on the dance floor with all the other kids while she waited for Sparky to come out, waving enthusiastically and joining in when she could even though Louise could see her legs were hurting from the exercise at the beach earlier. Louise had to space out her activities, so she wasn't over doing it.

She sat and watched as Lucy smiled and laughed in excitement when the different characters came on the stage singing and dancing. As tired as Louise was, watching Lucy in this moment made it worth it.

When the show ended, the disco began and Lucy stood up quick knowing the song "Firework" by Katy Perry, it was one of her favourites and Lucy went for it! She danced without inhibitions, shaking her head and mouthing to the

22

music as though she were singing; her delicate body carried along with her strong mind danced for four more songs until she stopped suddenly, sitting on the floor. Louise was ready with the buggy and picked Lucy up.

"Does it hurt?" Louise asked.

Lucy nodded and signed "hurt", she yawned, placing her head on Louise's shoulder.

"Ok, time to go to bed darling."

Lucy was asleep in minutes after ibuprofen for her aching muscles and Louise slowly sank into the soft cushions on the chair as Hayley passed her friend a full glass of wine.

"Bottoms up girl."

Louise took the drink gratefully and smiled as they clinked their glasses.

"Cheers" They both said.

It had been a full day. A good day, with a constant change of up and down situations as it always was with the kids. All four of them so different in some ways, yet similar in others; at times they would clash, and then beautiful moments would happen before their eyes causing the two friends to simply stop and marvel at how lucky they were to be here and know each other. They would share a look between them that showed the love they had for their children and happiness at the friendship they had found.

Other times, like the time in the pool (a different holiday), when Flynn had done a poo (And not just any poo, but the kind that would start leaking out the sides of the swimming nappy) and then into the water, was a bit of a tense situation. They had promised to stick together and help each other no matter what. It didn't matter they had only been in the pool for ten minutes, Hayley had to get Flynn out and changing his nappy was no easy task, he liked to wriggle and fight against it, which meant they all had to go. Louise couldn't keep three non-swimmers safe by herself so out they got, causing immediate crying from all four children.

The family sized changing room seemed small with the six of them crammed inside, Louise and Hayley struggling quietly to get the kids dry and dressed first, Hayley battling with Flynn's helicopter legs, the smell of poo thick in the air. Complete silence with the tension palpable as they worked to keep calm all the while the kids moaning and complaining.

"You ok?" Louise eventually spoke.

"Yep." Hayley answered tightly.

It wasn't until they were outside, had taken a deep breathe, looked at each other and then begun to laugh. They called it a test of their friendship; one wrong word could have easily sparked an argument between them.

"I've only got on one sock and I couldn't find my knickers." Hayley confessed, sending them in to peels of fresh laughter.

That was a few years ago now and they both sat laughing about it, sipping their wine.

"Oh, you never guess what I did today" Louise got up, refilling both their wine glasses.

"I swore, LOUD. In front of the kids."

Hayley laughed while Louise told her the story of the man coming towards her in the car.

"Well, he sounds like a fucking prick, so I make you right!"

"Amy actually told me off!" Louise looked shame faced.

"Oh, don't worry mate, it's not like you do that often is it. I mean you're so calm all the time; you deal with situations way better than I do. I wish I had your level head." Hayley said.

"I don't *feel* calm, inside my stomach is in knots, I'm trying not to lose it."

"Well, you hide it well. Great poker face." Hayley winked. "Seriously though, you shouldn't bottle that shit up it's not good for you and it does come out eventually. Usually when you don't expect it and at the wrong person. That's my trouble."

"Remember the pizza guy? The one you threw the bottle of coke at who was rude to you? I don't know how they still deliver to you I really don't." Louise chuckled.

"I hadn't slept for two days because of Flynn! He'd kept me up! And I apologised!" Hayley laughed at herself "Don't mess with a tired mum!"

"Or anybody who wrongly parks in a disabled bay eh mate?" Louise laughed at the memory. "Oh, that was so funny! That man's face when you shouted in his window... "are you disabled? You don't look disabled?! Where is your badge?!"

"It's true though! They shouldn't park there!" Hayley grinned remembering "And I had to make a big deal of walking Flynn past the car so they could see me struggling. They drove away then didn't they" Hayley thought for a moment "See I wish I could be more level-headed, you wouldn't have done that."

"No, your right I wouldn't, I would have stewed over it inside, putting me in a bad mood and it would have ruined our meal because it would be all I could have thought about, but no one would know. At least after you said your piece, he knew he was in the wrong and you felt better. I'd like to be more like you like that."

"It gets me in to trouble mate though sometimes, my big mouth."

Louise considered her friend for a moment then grinned as she agreed.

"Yeah. It is huge."

Hayley threw a pillow at her almost knocking over her wine.

"Hey! Watch it!"

The two friends laughed and talked for hours before heading to bed to wake up and do it all again.

CHAPTER THREE

Jenny Jones lay in bed wide awake, the crushing feeling on her chest like a physical pain. She lay there steadying her breathing for a long time and wished she could rip off the gremlin that continued to lay there, gripping the sides of her body, pressing down on her lungs. Her arms felt heavy, and her eyes itched from lack of sleep, she would need extra make up today to hide the dark circles. Sleep had been an impossible task, something she could never seem to catch no matter how hard or fast she ran after it, leaving her exhausted and now wide awake at 5.00 a.m. No point in trying any more, she may as well get up and get some jobs done. If she could only move...

The weight on her chest felt hard and heavy, she rubbed it with her hands wishing it away, her throat aching with tears that threatened to spill over and wake her sleeping husband. Jenny fought back the sobs that lay beneath the surface, always there waiting to come out.

She looked over at him with fondness, his low gentle snoring, somewhat comforting and took in his still handsome face. Chris was tall with an athletic build, his muscles on his ebony skin relaxed while he slept. Flecks of grey dotted through his once jet-black hair. His full lips slightly apart, she smiled at him. Her prince she used to call him, she hadn't for a while though. She didn't know why.

Jenny slowly rolled over to slide out of bed quietly, careful not to disturb him, her chest still heavy, taking deep breaths; on the fourth one she felt ready to stand, it was usually the fourth, on bad days it was more like 6 or 7.

Jenny crept out of the room thinking of the coffee she would need and the ironing that she hadn't done yesterday. That would keep her busy, and so it did. Once she began moving and focusing on her jobs, she couldn't feel the gremlin as much anymore.

By 7 am Jenny had finished the ironing, made the packed lunches for the kids, cleaned the downstairs bathroom and done her hair and make-up; Studying herself critically in the mirror, she looked for imperfections after applying her concealer and foundation. No, her skin looked ok, bit of blusher on her pale skin and mascara next. She straightened her naturally long blonde hair, curling the ends so they framed her face in a half curl. The person looking back at her did not resemble the person she felt inside. In the mirror she looked fresh and relaxed, inside she felt wooden.

Chris made her jump when he walked into the bathroom behind her.

"Hey. Good morning beautiful." He slid his arms around her, nuzzling her neck. Jenny stiffened a little, turning to peck him on the cheek before hurrying out of the bathroom.

"Good morning." Her breezy voice denied the emptiness she felt inside, the now all too familiar act of walking away from any form of contact with her husband, she tried not to notice his face fall as it so often did and instead hurried upstairs to wake the kids before cooking them all breakfast.

The twins were 5 and a half, boy and a girl. Paul and Mia; Perfect people said, you have one of each! And they were perfect, they were gorgeous. With the combination of Jenny's pale skin and Chris's African roots they were a beautiful blend of olive skin and thick curly black hair, their round chubby faces untouched by worry... young and innocent, they slept. Jenny woke them each with a kiss and within 10 minutes had them all at the breakfast table with fresh coffee for her and Chris, crumpets and cereal for the kids. Jenny intended to eat but just picked at the edge of her crumpet while the kids scooped up their cereal needing a little help now and again manipulating the spoon. Both Jenny and Chris would reach over to help them when they saw they needed to which went against the advice of the occupational therapist but neither could help it, how can you sit and watch your child struggle to eat and do nothing?

The twins had a global learning delay the professionals said. Everything was a little slower than it should be, to look at you wouldn't know anything was different and they *did* get looked at. A lot. If Jenny was on her own with them people would assume they weren't her children because of their colouring and naturally people stared because they were twins, when one of them would call her "Mummy." The starer would raise eyebrows in surprise and smile politely, saying something like "beautiful children.".

Being pregnant with twins was like an enormous celebration before they even arrived. People constantly congratulated them, especially with a boy and a girl... one of each! Perfect!

The birth had been horrendous, and Jenny had never gotten over it, although her figure had recovered nicely to her pre pregnant shape with thankfully no stretch marks at all, she had a c section scar in the shape of a huge cross on her stomach. The babies were in distress and stuck in abnormal positions, at some point they had been starved of oxygen which could be the cause of their learning delay; but they were lucky to be alive at all, two months premature, their first home being the baby neonatal care unit, weighing only 2 lbs each. Jenny had to leave them every day to the nurses to care for them overnight, her heart breaking each time, not able to celebrate the birth of their fragile babies because they weren't even home yet, weren't even ok yet and family would comment on her amazing shape that had 'bounced right back.' She had been unable to eat properly ever since they had been born, the constant uncertainty making her stomach reject any decent meal Chris tried to tempt her with. Jenny's wound was huge all across her stomach, red and ugly.

To her, it represented how she felt inside; sore and ugly. Her body not able to do its job to hold and feed her babies long enough to keep them safe and strong; strong enough to breathe alone when born, to feed from her instead of those clinical tubes keeping them alive, she pumped her milk religiously but even that was in vain, only small amounts would come and the pain of it pulled on her stomach, her wound sore and painful until she couldn't bear it anymore and eventually stopped trying, her milk drying up almost instantly like a relief of having to try to keep up the pretence that her body alone could care for these beautiful gifts she clearly didn't deserve to have.

What she could do, was smile and love them and be there every moment she was able to. She never rested; her wound becoming the consequence of that, which began to open and the infection that followed was a fresh reminder of how useless her body was.

The nurses that tended to her at the hospital, told her she must rest, or they would have to ban her from coming in. She was outraged.

"Those are my babies! I have to see them!"

Chris was taken into a side office while one of the nurses gently suggested Jenny may be a little depressed.

"I am not depressed." Jenny was not one to sit around and had overheard "My babies are in intensive care! My stomach is like a horror movie and I have to leave them every night and go home to an empty house! How dare you?!"

Despite the warnings from the doctor about resting, she went every day still but was more careful at home so her wound would heal. Two long months of waiting for her babies, of getting dressed each day alone in the bathroom so as to hide her scarred body from her husband, the constant reminder of her own failure, of walking in to the beautifully, impeccably decorated nursery, filled with everything a baby could ever wish for, teddies of every size and description, a rocking chair where she imagined sitting, rocking her babies feeding them in turn (a reminder that her breasts were unable to do that job) their gorgeous matching wooden cots with pink and blue bedding, the walls a light cream, curtains a pastel apple green, different soft colours delicately placed around the room. Jenny had read that colours were a stimulant for the brain, but harsh colours could overstimulate, so she chose carefully, and the result was a mix of soft pastels that brought it gently to life making it a happy place. It was meant to be a happy place, not empty and barren like Jenny now felt inside all the time.

When the babies finally came home, the celebrations they had planned with family and friends were replaced with regular check-ups with the consultant and health visitor. Jenny slowly built walls around her emotions so as to keep in control of herself and try to stop herself from sinking into this enormous black hole she found herself standing on the precipice of many times. It scared her, but she would focus on her babies, her wonderful babies who somehow had come into this world safely despite Jenny's useless body being able to protect them and house them until they were really ready to be born. They were a marvel when she thought about it and the love she felt when she held them was the only real thing she felt anymore and of course the fear. Fear that they would suddenly slip away as easily as they could have done that day they were born, how fragile they were, how easy it could have been... Fear that the doctors could be right when they said that premature twins could have developmental difficulties as they grew older, and it was impossible to tell at this stage if their traumatic birth had any kind of impact yet.

Traumatic birth. The words punctured Jenny's skin. Your fault, she heard. She knew it, they all knew it. The shame of it wore her down and she could only be grateful that they were here, and she could be their mother, and the best mother is what she would be, she vowed to herself and to them each and every day. They were always clean, Well dressed and on time. They worked through their speech cards every day and physio every day, Jenny cooked nourishing meals and had a strict routine, never deviating from it, read all the bedtime stories and attended the play dates, birthday parties, volunteered at the school on certain days, made the cakes for the bake sales, had a table on Christmas bazaars, she did everything she could and then some more, leaving very little room for anything else. Chris had begun to fade into the background a long time ago. She did love him, but she didn't know how on earth he could still love her. They used to be wildly passionate about each other, even their arguments were intense, now they didn't argue, they didn't talk about much at all really. They were just polite.

Chris had slowly begun to feel almost rude if he had tried to show his wife any kind of affection, she simply froze when he touched her and smiled at him while she found an excuse to move away until he stopped bothering altogether. There was a chasm between them that neither knew how to close anymore. The children were all they shared in common, and they devoted their lives to them.

"What are the plans for today?" Chris's voice broke into Jenny's thoughts.

"Well, after the school run, I have some shopping to do and a yoga class. How about you?"

"Work and then maybe the gym if you don't need me to come home earlier for anything." Chris chewed on his crumpets watching his beautiful wife sip her coffee and ignore her own breakfast.

"No that's fine, I don't need you home for anything. But dinner will be at six."

Jenny got up to start getting herself dressed for the day.

"Ok, I'll be home for six, what are you making?"

Jenny was half out of the room and turned distractedly at his question.

"What? Oh, spaghetti bolognaise and home-made garlic bread."

"Lovely. My favourite."

Jenny smiled politely "I know."

Chris watched her walk away again, sadness and loneliness encompassing him. Where had his wife gone? His best friend, his soul mate. He knew she didn't love him anymore but had moulded into this Stepford type wife that never put a foot wrong, always kept her voice to a nice tone; the house perfectly cleaned, his shirts always ironed, a decent meal on the table every single night and never asked for help. Not once. He had thought their move would help things, bring them together somehow; she wasn't connecting with anyone in their old area, close friends had become distant memories for her, nights out a thing of the past and they had wanted somewhere a little quieter than the busy London life they had been used to. Chris's job meant he could be flexible; he had worked hard over the years getting promotions until he was now the area bank manager, overseeing others manage their teams, being on call constantly. It was a demanding role but financially they were secure. Chris had suggested the move, thinking it would do them both good, a fresh start. He would notice Jenny staring at the nursery while Paul and Mia were still in the hospital, for hours sometimes. Only coming back to some kind of life when they came home but she had closed up, their fun and happy home suddenly turning quiet and sombre. They had been here a year and a half now but still Jenny kept people at arms length, keeping herself busy through the kids and not allowing herself any kind of a life.

 They used to be a team, would laugh endlessly at each other and make jokes, watch films, eat junk food and order takeaways, make love on the sofa or in the kitchen or the bathroom... they ignited each other in a way Chris had never felt, she completed him, and he missed her terribly.

CHAPTER FOUR

Louise glanced at her list, sighing deeply. She had two appointments for Lucy today. Two! In between two school runs when both of them were at different schools it seemed impossible, but she knew she would do it, probably give herself a stomach ulcer in the process but she would do it.

07:35. She was dressed and waiting for them to finish breakfast. Amy was quick at eating, but Lucy took forever, and every mouthful had to be encouraged.

Why did she agree to two appointments? Why didn't she just rearrange one?

Thinking ahead she would have to get Lucy on her bus so she could get Amy to school on time and speak to her teacher before she started school. Amy had a bit of an issue with a boy in her class, it had been going on about a week and she had chosen this morning to finally speak up. Pleased she had finally spoken up but irritated it was today of all days, Louise took a gulp of her coffee and practiced patience in her head while she watched Lucy chew as slow as humanly possible. 07:40.

She knew she could get Lucy dressed in minutes, five if she had to, so in between mouthfuls, Louise decided to get the packed lunches done and bags packed. Check all she needed was in her handbag already while Amy wrestled with her tights in the living room. Louise paused whizzing past to help her, then scooped some more food on to Lucy's spoon as she raced into the kitchen, clearing up as she went.

Louise was dressed, hair done and ready. Today was a day for make-up, she hadn't slept well, and it showed. She had been laying there worrying about how she would time it all and kicking herself for trying to be wonder woman and fit it all in, in one day.

07:50.

"Come on Lucy, how are you doing?" She tried to sound relaxed, but it came out agitated.

Lucy smiled up at her, her large eyes unaware of the angst occurring in her mum's stomach trying to keep to a timetable. Louise's posture deflated a little and she smiled back genuinely, and sat down again, loading more porridge on to her spoon. The feeding and swallowing team said she shouldn't do it for her but at 07:55 on a Tuesday morning, with Lucy still not dressed and the bus picking her up at 08:25, she would like to see them stick to that rule!

"Come on darling two more." Louise encouraged as Amy came over to get her hair brushed.

"Mum I have knots." She whined.

Amy's beautiful curls came at a price and that price was knots. No matter how tightly Louise tried to keep it tied back of an evening the kid must do an Irish dance on her head in the night because somehow it always escaped and there, they were fighting the tangles each and every morning, Amy whining and trying to move away.

"You can't go to school with your hair in a mess and knotty Amy, come on."

"But whhyyyyy?" Amy whined.

"Because it doesn't look nice that's why." Louise fought the curls and eventually won; Amy not happy about the process at all.

Ok, hair done, well Amy's anyway, packed lunches done, Amy was dressed...

"Put your shoes on please Amy. Amy, Amy!"

"Huh?" Amy's gaze reluctantly left the TV screen, Louise momentarily remembered the parents who didn't allow screen time in the morning. She envied those parents and fleetingly wondered if their mornings were a happy breeze flowing naturally as they all left for school on time, and of course all looking perfect as they did so.

Amy busied herself with her shoes while Louise took Lucy to the toilet and to have the quickest change in history. 08:05.

By 08:15 Lucy was ready with shoes on, so was Amy. It was a warm day so only cardigans were needed. Louise threw all the breakfast bits in the sink, made sure she had her appointment letters in her handbag and then stepped in cat sick.

"Ahhhh Ewwww! Oh no!"

"What's wrong mum?" Amy came into see what was wrong.

"I stepped in cat sick!" As Louise tried to hop past the front door to go and wash her foot, the door knocked.

"They're early!" She groaned "Hang on! Come on Lucy Locket, let's go darling."

Balancing on one foot and pulling Lucy up, she got her to the front door with her school bag and packed lunch.

"Mum that's MY packed lunch."

"What? Oh of course it is silly me!" Louise passed Amy her packed lunch back and picked up the other one, opening the door.

"Hi Maureen, how are you?" Louise found the more she was stressed, the higher her voice became when speaking to this woman.

"Good morning." Maureen was about fifty, with ash brown hair and a face that looked like she didn't smile very much at all. But she smiled at Lucy and that's all that Louise cared about.

Louise put Lucy's hand in Maureen's.

"Is it ok If I don't walk out today, we are running a bit behind." Louise hid her cat sick foot behind her other leg.

"Yes, that's ok." Maureen began to walk off.

"Hang on!" Louise had to hop out the door then to kiss Lucy goodbye, to hell with it, she could think what she likes.

"Love you, see you soon."

"Love oo, bye." Lucy waved.

"Lucy has appointments today." Louise called after Maureen who clearly didn't want to waste another second. "And so, she won't be coming home on the bus and I have her buggy."

"Ok." The woman replied not turning around.

Louise watched them walk down the path on one leg as the cat sick had started to dry on her feet, in between her toes too and wished she was able to take Lucy to school as well instead of having to rely on strangers to take her in and pick her up every day. They seemed nice enough... to Lucy, but it changed every term, was confusing for her and Louise wanted to be able to have that connection with the school that she had with Amy's too. In some ways it was more important because she needed that extra communication not that she liked saying one was more important then the other, that is not what she meant...

08:20

"Shit."

Louise raced upstairs to clean her foot, two minutes later she was almost ready, the fluttering in her chest beginning to settle as she felt in control again.

"Can we take my bike today please mum?"

Louise literally had her hand on the door.

"But it's in the shed... we don't have time..."

Amy's face looked immediately crushed "But it's bike week, we couldn't yesterday because we didn't have time and there's a chart at school..."

Louise breathed deeply "Ok, how about this? We put your bike in the car, drive halfway to school and then you bike the rest?"

Amy's face lit up again and nodded enthusiastically.

"Great, come on let's go!"

The bike and Lucy's buggy were a bit of a squeeze in the car, but thankfully the big boot was able to manage it. Amy's Happy face while riding to school was worth it. She turned the corner as all parents were piling through across the green from the carpark, from the zebra crossing, in different directions; time to slow down, they were almost here and not late. Louise smiled serenely as though her morning had been an easy one while she spied other mums appearing the same way. Stepping into a calm she put on for pretence and a confidence she didn't feel, Louise merged into the traffic of parents following their children.

"Better get off now babe, there's a lot of people."

Amy hopped off her bike so Louise could push it along now. There was a rule once you were inside the school gates you couldn't ride your bike or scooter. Amy had been right, there were lots of kids on bikes or scooters, some on skateboards; some Mums had joined them, and they had biked together, complete with matching helmets too, Amy noticed too.

"Mum why don't you ride a bike to school with me?"

"Because I don't have one."

"Why?"

"Because they're too expensive darling."

"I've got some pocket money; I will buy you a bike."

Louise slowed down to put her arm around Amy, smiling warmly "Oh you are so sweet you really are. I love you."

"I love you too Mum, but I want you to have a bike, then we can go out together."

"It's just... It's not easy for me to ride a bike with Lucy."

"Oh, right yeah." Amy understood then. Lucy couldn't ride a bike and couldn't be left so Louise could go and ride a bike with Amy. Louise felt guilty then. Guilty she couldn't do these things and make those special moments and guilty that she sometimes resented that she couldn't, then guilty she felt it in the first place!

"But I *love* watching you ride your bike ever so grown up, you're so good at it too."

"Am I?"

"Absolutely. Far better than I ever was."

They had reached the entrance now, there was a bit of a walk right round to the back of the building to Amy's class, second week into year 1 and so far, so good. Amy loved learning and was a kind, gentle girl, she made friends easily but got hurt easily too, it was her nature, she was open and trusting. Louise loved that about her but worried about it too, especially when this issue had come up this morning; this boy Andrew had taken a bit of a shine to Amy and had been following her around all last week, Amy wasn't comfortable with it when he started trying to kiss her and so had turned to trying to trip her up now instead after she had told him to stop.

"What are you going to say Mum?" Amy looked worried.

"Just that Andrew needs to learn the right way to play with people." Louise bent down to face Amy "Don't worry, I will say it in a nice way OK? But he has to stop bothering you and if we don't talk about it then teachers don't know and can't help."

"OK Mummy."

"Go on, you go through now and I'll talk to your teacher, I love you and I'll see you after school."

"Can I ride my bike home too?"

"Yes of course." Louise mentally working out how she will push Lucy in her buggy to the school run while bringing the bike... she really needed to buy a bike chain to leave it at the school.

"Love you Mum."

"Love you too, have a great day."

Louise watched Amy filing through the door holding her packed lunch and felt her shoulders start to relax. School run number 2 almost complete.

"Mr Knowles" Louise called before he disappeared back into the classroom. "Could I have a word with you please?"

Mr Knowles listened and nodded to Louise explain the issue between Amy and Andrew, agreeing to speak to him and tell him to leave Amy alone.

"I would also like it mentioned to his parents please."

Mr Knowles looked surprised.

"Oh, well why don't we see how it works out this way first?" He suggested.

"The boy is trying to trip up my daughter because she won't kiss him, his parents need to be aware of it." Louise was cold, her demeanour rigid. This was a grown man she didn't need to be soft with him "It's not acceptable." Louise added.

Mr Knowles nodded quickly, realising Louise wasn't at all happy about the situation.

"It has taken her over a week to speak up and she needs to know that when she speaks up for help, things change for the better otherwise what sort of message does that send to a young girl?"

"Oh! Yes definitely! Yes of course." Mr Knowles couldn't argue when Louise put it to him like that.

"Thank you. Goodbye."

"Goodbye Mrs Barker."

"MISS Barker." Louise corrected.

09:05, an hour until the first appointment, Louise could slow down a bit.

"Hey! How are you? How was your holiday?"

Katie breathed heavily catching up to Louise as she wheeled Amy's bike out of the school gates. Katie lived down Louise's road, they spoke sometimes on the school run but that was about it, they weren't exactly friends. Actually, Katie irritated Louise a little; she was quite full of herself, always had something nasty to say about someone and Louise was sure she had probably been on the receiving of it at times; Katie just seemed to enjoy discussing other people's lives, making her think she couldn't exactly be happy with her own.

"You're a bit late today aren't you, that's not like you?" Katie asked.

"Yeah, just one of those mornings... and will probably be one of those days." She smiled wryly.

Katie popped a cigarette in her mouth and lit it, blowing smoke in the air as if she had been holding her breath for a long time.

"So... the holiday?" Katie asked again, tucking her cigarette packet into her low-cut top so it balanced between her big boobs. Louise fought the very strong urge to roll her eyes at this so obviously attention seeking gesture and answered her instead,

"It was great." She said honestly "We had a wonderful time." Louise smiled fondly at all the new memories they had made.

"Aww that's so sweet." Katie dragged on her cigarette "You went with your friend, didn't you? Must be so hard on your own, at least I have Brian to help, even if he is a total dick at times."

"No not really. We have our own routine and it's actually quite nice not having to think of looking after another person or clearing up after them or listening to all their bullshit."

Katie opened her mouth to respond, but Louise cut her off, she couldn't take another barbed comment from her today.

"Anyway, got to run, have a real busy day ahead. Bye!"

Louise dashed for the car, pulling Amy's bike along with her. She actually had plenty of time before getting Lucy for her first appointment, but she couldn't stand that woman! She was always looking for someone to cut down with her nasty comments, constantly talked about herself and looked down on other people. Louise found her toxic, she could zap your energy in a second without you realising.

"Come on Simon, we are SO late!"

Louise looked up to see a woman literally running down in the road, she had clearly just gotten out of bed and thrown jogging bottoms over the top of pyjama's but still wearing slippers, her hair hadn't seen a brush yet and behind her was an untidy boy trying to stuff his white shirt into his trousers as he ran along behind her. It made Louise smile, but not unkindly, she knew most mums had a nightmare each morning sticking to times and schedules and the worst thing is if anyone oversleeps. The panic is horrible, and she felt for the woman running down the road in her slippers, knowing Katie would be sneering when she saw her.

Louise put the bike in the car ready to take home, then realised there wouldn't be time because if Amy wanted to ride her bike home and Lucy's second appointment was at 1:30 she would be cutting it very fine. Ok so the bike stays in the car.

The engine growled to life, music filling the car, she could now change the channel to the one she wanted at her level. Amy didn't like loud music, Lucy liked it so she could feel it pumping through her body and Louise was somewhere in the middle. By the time she got to Lucy's school she still had 20 minutes to wait before she needed to get her, she could have kept her off with the morning appointment, it would have been much easier but because she had so many appointments the school liked her to come in for her morning mark first and Louise wasn't one to argue with the school unless she had to. She sat there and relaxed, picking up her phone and began to scroll through Facebook as she waited.

A picture of Hayley with her arms around the boys came up when they were at the caravan. Her big smile reaching her eyes, crinkling at the corners, she looked relaxed and happy. Louise remembered the exact moment that picture had been taken. They were at the caravan just having had lunch, already been swimming so they all had swimming hair and Flynn had been very affectionate all morning; he loved holidays, it really brought him out of himself and swimming was one of his favourite things to do. Louise remembered Hayley feeling so happy because Flynn was so happy, he had come over for an unexpected hug, so Hayley had grabbed Sam while she had the opportunity and Louise took the picture. It was a great picture of them all, natural and beautiful. A real holiday snap.

Louise liked the photo and commented underneath.

"Great photo of you all mate, wish we were still there XXX".

The memory had made Louise smile and she continued to scroll through all the different faces and lives on her screen. Then she stopped as she saw a new one from Jenny; it was a picture of Paul and Mia on their first day back after the summer, starting year 1. They were on the doorstep in their uniforms; not a hair out of place, beautiful kids they really were. Gorgeous olive skin and curly dark hair. She had braided Mia's hair, adding yellow ribbon to the ends, it must have taken hours Louise thought as she looked at the photo. They had lovely smiles and posed perfectly for their photo. Underneath was a second one of them as a family next to the fireplace, it must have been taken on a timer because all four of them were in it, Jenny on the left, the twins in the middle and slightly in front and Chris on the right. Chris and Jenny had their arms around each other's waist and the other resting on one of the twins in front. All impeccably dressed, the twins wore their uniform so must have been the same morning and Jenny wore a grey pencil skirt accentuating her lovely figure, white blouse and black low heels. Her naturally long blonde hair twisted into a loose ponytail, her make up just right. Chris wore black trousers and a blue shirt, slightly open at the collar. They looked incredible all standing together around their open fireplace, like a picture out of a magazine (Which Louise was slightly jealous of), but something wasn't right about Jenny, her smile was kind of frozen, practiced. Chris too.

She pondered over the photo for a moment, the seemingly perfect photo before pressing like and commenting how lovely they all looked as a family, reminding herself to get in touch with Jenny and see how she was doing. It wasn't easy moving to a new area and making new friends. Even if you did have the big house, nice car, husband with the great job at the bank... you still needed friends.

CHAPTER FIVE

Hayley could smell it the second she opened her eyes. No, *before* she opened her eyes. In fact, it was what woke her up, she was so sensitive to the smell but should be so used to it by now. She picked up her phone 04:37.

"Fuck sake" She groaned.

She would never get back off to sleep now and if she laid here the smell would get worse and she would still have to deal with it in an hour or so, but as soon as she was up, she knew the demands would start. It had only been a few moments, but Hayley knew sleep was impossible now as the job ahead loomed in her mind, whipping off the covers in one fluid motion she got up. Her bedroom door was open and so was Flynn's right next door. She did this on purpose so she knew when he needed changing, if it was left it just went everywhere and the smell was so strong... or maybe she had developed such a dislike for it, the moment she could smell it she was on alert.

Hayley walked into Flynn's room and could cry at the sight and even stronger smell of poo in the room. He had taken his nappy off this time and thrown it probably, making it half stick to the wall, where he had shuffled out of bed, all his sheets were covered in it and he was sitting naked playing happily with his woody doll. He loved his woody doll, was swinging it round and round and round by its arm singing to it in a happy tune only Flynn knew the words to, looking up at the ceiling.

Hayley cleaned Flynn first, so she could cuddle him after, but Flynn wasn't in a cuddly mood, he pushed her away looking at the ceiling.

"Ok Flynn, I'll put the telly on for you, be back soon." Hayley put the tv on in the living room and went to tackle the bed sheets and clean the wall. Half an hour later the room was fresh and clean again, sheets in the washing machine and a Yankee candle lit to hide the lingering smell. Switching the kettle on, it was time for coffee; she needed it this morning.

Walking into the living room to settle down with Flynn for a little while with her coffee, Hayley sat down but Flynn had decided he wanted breakfast having been up longer than anyone else, he was already hungry.

"Eat." Flynn signed.

"Ok Flynn, one waffle or two?" Hayley put her hands up to show the choices for him and he high fived the two choice. Happiness burst through her at the engagement he showed before he went back to spinning round on the spot humming his personal tune. Hayley smiled at him from the kitchen. Happy in his own world, Flynn was a beautiful boy, innocent and unaffected by others as long as his routine was consistent and his needs were met, he was happy, but he did like things his own way and was particular in how that was. She stayed in the kitchen until the waffles were ready, if she tried to sit down, Flynn would think she wasn't cooking them and get frustrated.

Hayley looked out of the window. They lived in a nice neighbourhood. The sun was coming up now, the birds had slowly begun their tunes and the sky was turning a pinkie colour. She watched it getting lost in the colours and shapes in the clouds when the toaster binged, and it was time to turn the waffles over. Flynn heard the bing, sliding over to the kitchen on his bum, peering round the door.

"Not yet Flynn, one more time then they'll be ready."

They lived in a modern ground floor flat, she liked being on one level, it made it so much easier to take care of the boys by herself and she had been by herself for quite a while now. In fact, Sam had never even met his dad. Michael walked out while she was pregnant with him, still getting used to Flynn's needs who was only a year at the time, he walked out. Not a word since. The odd child support here and there, but that was him all over, sporadic and never reliable. But charming when he wanted to be. He was probably charming his way into someone else's life right now. Bastard.

She had done it all, alone and was still doing it. His loss. They were amazing kids. Sam was like a little best friend; they would play games, watch films and muck about endlessly, snuggle up together when they both felt lonely or sad and were in tune with each other. She wished so hard for the same with Flynn and it had taken a long time to realise that it just wasn't the way he was, but she struggled to accept it, taking each choice he made to be solitary personally, and it hurt. It hurt a lot.

"It's ready Flynn." She called in a sing song voice, he liked her tone when she did that and would put his head to the side and smile. Shuffling over on the shiny wooden floors Hayley had saved for and was so proud of, he made his way over to the table for his morning waffles.

43

The coffee had kicked in so while Flynn was eating, Hayley tidied up, not that there was much to tidy, she was great at keeping on top of the cleaning (Flynn was awake until late and up early so it kept her busy instead of watching the TV).

She planned for the dinner that evening, cleaned the bathroom, polished the living room and decided to do her hair and make-up. It was only 06:30 and the bus came for Flynn at 08:30. Flynn had disappeared back into his bedroom again, so Hayley got him dressed for school. Flynn didn't always like getting dressed and would move away, little jerky movements that were surprisingly strong, Hayley would often get a leg in her stomach, once he got her full on in the neck.

Hayley took Flynn's lycra suit down, taking deep breaths as she did. She hated this bit, so did he. It was so tight, but the occupational therapist told her it was good for his muscles and movement, sending signals to his brain as if to 'Wake up' his muscles and use them more. Getting it on was a real mission, especially where he wouldn't keep still.

Flynn began to moan as Hayley pulled on the legs of the suit. It came to just below his knees, and just past his elbows like a wetsuit really. She had to try to get it over his nappy as well which wasn't easy. After a lot of tugging, pulling and jiggling, Flynn was in his suit. Neither of them was happy about it. Hayley's heart was racing, and she was hot now too. Flynn pulled away from her, an accusing look in his eyes. She hated this. Trying to do her best for him and putting him through that each morning when he clearly hated it but if it was best for him, she had to didn't she?

Hayley tried to give Flynn a hug after, but he immediately pushed her away, needing his own space now. Tears pricked her eyes at the rejection. She had so much love to give him and he never wanted it, never gave it back. Didn't need that emotional bond. He was happy in his world and that's where he wanted to be. Alone.

Hayley left him then, feeling low and tired. She loved him so much, she wanted so badly to hug and kiss her son and talk to him, read to him, watch tv with him but he batted her away, preferring to always be alone.

"Morning Mum." Sam sleepily put his arms round her waist for a hug and she held him there tight, fighting back her tears, not wanting to let him go.

"I'm hungry."

"Morning babe, cereal?"

"Yes please." Sam smiled up at her and she felt better. Chatting to him about his day, Hayley begun his breakfast and orange juice, preparing his packed lunch for the day.

They laughed together over Sam's cartoon he was watching, and Hayley saw Flynn close his door, he didn't like any noise but his own. Trying not to let it bother her she sat with Sam while he ate.

"Right, buddy It's time to get dressed now." Hayley told Sam as she finished her own breakfast of toast.

"Ok Mum." Sam jumped down and run off to get ready. He liked school, that made things easier really. The only drama was when another kid upset him or there was a teacher he didn't like, but that didn't happen often really. He was sensitive though, to Hayley's emotions and loved being with her. He missed her when he was at school and she missed him too, but the days flew by while she worked out her frustrations at the gym or pounding the pavement with her music throbbing in her ears; It made her feel alive, tired out her muscles and calmed her overactive brain, she needed exercise like other people needed addictions like cigarettes, chocolate or coffee. If Hayley couldn't exercise for a few days, it was like she would carry around all this pent-up energy she didn't know how to get rid of. It would bubble on the surface until someone said or did the wrong thing and she would blow. Last time it was the young guy who had parked in the disabled bay at McDonalds with his music pumping out of his open windows while he sat to eat his burger. Hayley had taken Flynn by the hand and walked right up to his window (Louise and the girls were there too, Louise's head in her hands as she saw what was about to unfold).

"Are you disabled?" Hayley's loud, irritated voice filled his ears and rang around the carpark "You don't LOOK disabled, and I don't see a badge."

Hayley had only just started "I've had to park all the way over there..." Pointing to the back of the car park "And walk my DISABLED SON all this way because of YOU!"

The young guy revved his engine and drove away immediately not even finishing his burger, shame and embarrassment flashing across his cheeks.

"Well, that did the trick." Louise commented walking over with the girls "Did you want to move your car?"

"Nah, I just wanted to make my point." Hayley grinned "I feel better now."

Cleaning helped her too, she cleaned houses while the boys were at school. She was good at it too, had a sharp eye for things and worked quickly. It tired her body and soothed her mind; she would be ready to relax with the boys at the end of the day when they came home from school. Today she had the gym, she needed it.

Hayley was getting dressed in her gym leggings and top when she thought she could smell it again. No, it can't be. It's just my imagination she thought, just in my head. Deciding to check anyway, Hayley pushed open Flynn's door and groaned. The smell hitting her as she took in the sight in front of her.

Flynn had done another poo, but this time it was a loose one and with the tightness of the lycra suit it had been pushed right up the back of his nappy and around his neck. Flynn couldn't get the suit off and so it had spread on to his clothes as well. It was 07:45, at least she had time still, because there was nothing left to do but a bath. Hayley stripped Flynn in the bath being as quick as she could while he fought every movement, poo was everywhere and the smell strong. Thankfully she had another uniform ready for him, but the suit would have to be left until it was washed and dry, they only had one and she didn't think she could cope with putting it on again even if it was clean. Flynn loved baths and moaned when he couldn't stay in it longer, confused to the change in his routine. His nightly baths were a pleasure for both of them, he would sing and play with his toys, Hayley watching him with pride as he let her stay and add a few light up sensory mood floaters to the bath, turning the big light off he would laugh. It was one of their moments they shared and loved. But today was not a night-time bath it was a quick bath and Flynn bucked and rocked, shouting at her while she tried to get him out after he was clean.

"Come on Flynn, you can have another one later." Trying hard to keep her voice sing song.

"Mum where's my shoes?" Sam was half dressed and wandering around looking for them.

Hayley had begun to sweat, her heart pulsing loudly in her ears. She was stressed now, trying to keep things light despite all that had happened this morning she wrapped Flynn in a big towel and dried him, while he fought her.

"Ahhhhhhhh" Flynn moaned loudly, rocking to get away from her. He was so strong!

"Come on Flynn we need to get dressed for school." Her sing song voice turning shrill under the pressure of having fifteen minutes until the bus arrived with that irritating woman who always *had* to comment on Hayley's appearance.

"Mum where's my shoes?" Sam repeated, still wandering around, shirt untucked, and buttons not lined up. Hayley glanced at him quickly seeing she would need to help him too. How had this happened? How could she have been up so God damn early and now be this stressed and up against it for time?

"Mum-?"

"I DON'T KNOW!" She shouted, "GO LOOK!"

"Come on Flynn! We have to get dressed now!"

Hayley didn't know how she managed to get every new item of uniform on before the bus arrived in the carpark outside, bibbing it's horn loudly but she did. With seconds to spare. Flynn was truly upset now, having had to get dressed twice and not wanting any physical contact at all. Hayley tried desperately to hug him or kiss him, to give him any kind of affection but he wouldn't even look at her. It was like a punch to the stomach, she wanted to cry and couldn't. The bus was outside. Normally after getting ready in the morning, Flynn would have his break in his room and was ready for the next part of the morning which was walking out in the carpark with Hayley. He needed those breaks, his routine was so important, it had to be a certain way for him, or he would get so upset. Hayley knew this, all his ways and couldn't bear to see him this way. But with the poo explosion which he did get from time to time, a bath was the only way to go, there simply weren't enough wet wipes left in the world otherwise, but that screwed up his routine in his head.

Flynn wouldn't let Hayley pick him up now, so she had to get him in his buggy to take him out, feeling the minutes tick by as the bus waited, she grew silent trying to stay calm.

"Found my shoes Mum." Sam announced as Hayley finally went through the door to meet the escort waiting at the bus.

"Morning!" She announced brightly. Grinning stupidly at Hayley.

It was morning four hours ago Hayley thought as she chose to ignore her today.

"Ooh you look flushed my dear. Are you ok? And what's wrong with Flynn this morning? Not very happy?" Her wheedling tone irritated Hayley. Her palm itched, wanting to slap the stupid woman. Couldn't someone see a bad morning when they saw one?

"Does he look happy?" Hayley snapped.

"No, that's w-"

"Then he's not fucking happy is he!" Hayley helped Flynn on the bus, clicking his seatbelt into place, her heart heavy and low. Tears threatening any moment. Not now. Not now.

Flynn stopped wriggling and moaning for just a second then, he didn't look at Hayley, but just past her, putting his hand in to her hair feeling the texture of it. Something he liked to do; it was like his way of a hug.

Hayley's throat choked, the tears spilled over now, unstoppable. She kissed his cheek and he allowed it.

"I love you Flynn" She managed to get out, not caring they were waiting, that Sam was inside getting flustered about being late for school probably, that the escort was still smarting for being sworn at; She was having a moment with Flynn. They were so unexpected, rare and fleeting that when they came you had to stop and enjoy it.

"Are you ok love?" The woman tentatively asked, in a softer tone when Hayley withdrew from the bus.

"Bad day." Hayley whispered as she turned to go back inside to get Sam to school on time, she wiped her tears, took a breath and fixed her smile in place ready to face the other school mums.

CHAPTER SIX

Louise slowly clicked the doors to the girl's bedrooms closed, after checking they were asleep. She loved checking on them at night, when the madness of the day was done, they had gotten through another day and there they lay in their cotton pyjamas, sweetly sleeping, making the faintest of sounds. Perfect. Their gorgeous innocent faces untouched by troubles. Louise wanted it to always be that way for them. She would stand there for five minutes sometimes not able to believe how lucky she was and wishing she hadn't rushed the bath time as much as she had or the dinner time or the bedtime story, but she was tired by that time and just needed some quiet. The sound of the nearby train passing by was all she could hear from outside. Her road was pretty quiet, you only walked that way if you lived there or to cut through to the park and this time of night nobody was going to the park. It was a quiet area, they were lucky, she thought again. Louise looked at the girls, an ache forming in her chest. She had no-one to share this moment with, as much as she had longed for bedtime earlier, now it was here, loneliness engulfed her, and an unexpected sadness overcame her. She blew them both a kiss, worried if she did kiss their soft cheeks, she would wake them.

Tip toeing downstairs, Louise went straight into the kitchen to pour a glass of wine. It was only Tuesday she chastised herself but after two appointments in one day plus the usual juggling she felt she had earned it.

Louise checked her phone as she plonked herself on the sofa cradling the cool glass and taking her first sip. A message from Hayley flashed on the screen.

Hayley: Hey babe! How's your day been? X

Louise: Mental. You? X

Hayley: Not great to be honest, been up since the crack of dawn with Flynn. He threw his nappy again at the wall. It was everywhere, then after a long morning I put his suit on and he done another loose one so was everywhere. He had a melt down after a bath and I almost had one too X.

Louise: Oh mate! You ok? X

Hayley: I'm fine, I just feel so awful, it was so hard. It's so hard sometimes X.

Louise: I know XXX

Louise: Do you want me to call? X

Hayley: No babe, I don't feel like talking. Thanks anyway X.

Louise: Ok. What did you have for dinner? X

Hayley: Needed an easy one so just jacket potatoes tonight with cheese and beans, what did you have? X

Louise: Easy dinners are the best! We had leftover lasagne and wedges, ate far too much as usual! X

Hayley: Lol! You can afford to! You having a wine tonight? X

Louise: How did you know?! X

Hayley: Me too, shouldn't really. I should wait 'til the weekend but sod it X.

Louise: Cheers X

Hayley: Cheers X

They chatted for two hours by text, ignoring the TV and listening to one another open up about their day. It helped, it usually did. By the time they said goodnight, both were feeling much better. Cementing the plans for Saturday they had agreed to do soft play this week, then McDonalds after. Louise climbed into bed, much more relaxed now after two large glasses of wine and talking to Hayley. Tomorrow was another day.

CHAPTER SEVEN

The temperature outside had dropped, the streets speckled with orange and yellow leaves as they danced their way down from the trees. Autumn was here. Jenny loved Autumn, everything was beautiful and crisp. Halloween wasn't far away, the kids loved it, dressing up, the sweets, dressing the house and being outside in the dark.

Jenny watched mesmerised as the leaves fell, one by one. She imagined them as a summer day; each one representing a fun day full of laughter, of days in the park, in the paddling pool, family barbecue's, all summer things floating away until next year when the tree would grow new leaves and new days would come. The end of summer. Jenny was so focused on the tree it was all she could see, her coffee forgotten as she stood there watching the leaves fall. She imagined laughter as each leaf dropped from its branches and smiled as she thought of the twins in their paddling pool, she smiled remembering them splashing about in their pool, laughing, their gorgeous little bodies more tanned than usual from the summer sun, the smell of sun cream in the air. Something was wrong; when Paul splashed Mia, the water stained her body turning it red. She cried. Jenny tried to call out, something in the air had changed, it wasn't a fun summers day any longer. The twins were crying, the pool was filled with blood not water, the pool was closing in on them and Jenny couldn't reach them. She couldn't get there, she was trapped by the window, she watched as the pool encased the twins who were now babies again, the pool had become her womb. Jenny banged fruitlessly on the window, words a prisoner in her throat as she tried to scream for them, but the image locked in a leaf and fell to the ground, tears and cries replacing the laughter until the whole tree shook with grief as the leaves fell from it. Jenny stepped back from the window, her coffee spilling from her cup, red liquid pouring on to the carpet, red? Blood? Soon she was running from it, her feet slow and sticky...

Jenny lay completely still trying to control her breathing, her heart racing as her eyes adjusted to the thick black room. Her recurring nightmare was just as frightening as the first day she had had it, she knew what it represented; Her failure to keep her babies safe inside of her, she didn't need a shrink to tell her that. She just hoped one day they would stop. She stole a glance at Chris, he was asleep thankfully, she hadn't disturbed him this time. He had to be up and fresh for work.

Jenny looked at the digital clock on her nightstand, the numbers announcing 4:34. She would never get back off to sleep now and so slowly slipped out of bed, sliding the sheets away from her quietly. She padded softly downstairs careful not to wake anyone, she was particularly good at tiptoeing around quietly in the morning after years of practice. Jenny crept into the kitchen and switched on the kettle, making her coffee a little stronger this morning. She didn't have any ironing to do, the house was already clean, maybe she could prepare a casserole for tonight but then what would she do today? She found herself in front of the living room window looking out at the sleeping street. The trees were dropping their leaves just like in her dream but this time it was different; you couldn't see the colours, just black and grey hues and shadows cast from the streetlight. There was a large Oak tree across the road just like in her dream, beautifully big and full. Its branches spread out like arms holding a bounty of life. She watched as the leaves flittered downwards, each leaf a memory of summer days lost. She checked her cup, there was still just coffee there.

"Hey." Chris's voice woke her from her thoughts. She jolted around, unused to being disturbed this time of the morning.

"Hi." Jenny immediately realised how terrible she must look. Chris stood there, looking a little rumpled in his blue shorts, but otherwise still the same gorgeous husband she had fallen head over heels for.

"Did I wake you? I'm sorry-"

"It's ok, I just woke up and wondered where you were. Are you ok? It's early Jen."

The truth was he woke up when she had thrashed about moaning, her breath quickening, increasing with her rising panic until she was loudly panting each breath and her eyes snapped open. He had watched her, tried to hold her hand, to soothe her from her recurring dream like he had done for years. She was so closed off to him these days he knew she wouldn't want him seeing her like that so always pretended to be asleep when she finally woke from her nightmares grasp.

"I'm ok. Just…" Jenny glanced out the window not knowing what to say, she felt vulnerable and silly. The tree released more leaves, dropping them to the ground to curl up and turn crisp.

"Halloween." She announced.

"What?" Chris asked a bit confused.

"It will be Halloween soon, we have to buy pumpkins, and squash for the soup. New costumes for the kids, get the decorations from the loft. There's a lot to do."

"We have about a week and a half babe, that's plenty of time."

"And I want to make gingerbread witches for the school and bats too, maybe a cake. I guess it's just on my mind that's all."

Chris smiled "I can help you know; you don't have to do it all on your own."

"You're busy with work."

"Not that busy that I can't help with Halloween. How about this weekend we go get the pumpkins together? We can pick our own from the farm." Chris suggested.

"Ok, that would be nice." Jenny put her cup down, suddenly feeling tired.

Chris wanted to put his arms around her, he got batted away so often he never knew when he could or should try, he so wanted to comfort her and found himself walking towards her. She didn't back away, just fixed her eyes on the carpet, lost in thought. Chris embraced her, his warm malleable body wrapped around her rigid one, she couldn't respond but leaned into him closing her eyes accepting the hug. She hadn't pushed him away and they stood there for the longest time, Chris holding her and smelling her hair, relishing the rare moment he got to hold his wife, feeling her unspoken pain and wishing he could make it stop.

CHAPTER EIGHT

"Amy, hold on!" Louise tried to keep up, almost getting stuck in the plastic tunnel that was *not* made for adults, twisting in ways that her 35-year-old body did not want to twist anymore. She really must start doing yoga Louise thought fleetingly as she was reminded yet again how unsupple she was trying to bend her way through the blue tunnel to keep up with Sam and Amy.

"You're so slow Mum!" Amy and Sam laughed at Louise.

"Did we *have* to go this way?"

"Yes, it's the best way." Sam said watching Louise wriggle uncomfortably out of the tube in a very unladylike fashion, landing heavily on her back. Louise stole a glance down below to see how Hayley was doing with Lucy and Flynn and saw her friend laughing openly at her.

"Thankyou." She mouthed which made Hayley laugh even more.

Soft Play Mania was a place they enjoyed going, it had everything for them, smaller separate areas for the babies, then a middle bit for the small toddlers and then the big, padded climbing frame filled with tunnels and slides for the slightly older kids or those who could climb. It was all set out in such a way that from each area you could clearly see each section and it wasn't too big that if you nipped to the toilet it wouldn't take long to spot the kids in the climbing frame afterwards. The cafe was situated along the wall in the middle with round tables dotted about in front of the play areas. It was just right for them. Amy and Sam were able to climb around the larger frame easy enough, but Louise and Hayley still liked to follow them round for the first hour to make sure they were ok and to check out who else was there, you could spot a troublemaker a mile away in those places, and sometimes it got so hectic, older kids would come in and run riot, pushing the little ones out of the way. Best to follow them for a bit.

Kids screaming excitedly, some screaming unhappily, babies crying, toddlers and older children crying, laughing, parents constantly calling out for their child, party music fighting to drown it all out and the kitchen staff shouting out their orders while staff and parents wandered around trying to find the correct table number with their arms laden with food or looking for their child to sit at their table with their hot lunch becoming cold. It was manic and the sounds meshed together into a background noise you just kind of got used to.

Louise, Sam and Amy finally got to the top of the yellow slide, this was the bigger slide of the two and they both loved going down it, but it had taken a while for their confidence to catch up with their intentions, but now they would go down it over and over. Hayley got so excited the first time it happened and raced over to Louise who had been with Lucy and Flynn spinning them round on the pole, they both loved that.

"They've done it! They've gone down the big slide!" Hayley had announced, grinning from ear to ear before running back to them to watch them do it again. Or more likely to go down the slide again herself, she loved getting involved and enjoyed every second of their success. Louise loved that about her, her energy was infectious and lifted you instantly, but she was real too. Probably the most honest person she had ever met, maybe too honest sometimes with certain people, especially if they pissed her off, but that was Hayley, you couldn't change her and Louise wouldn't want to, not for the world.

"Come on you two let's go on three. One, two, three!" Louise, Sam and Amy pushed off and flew down the slide for the twentieth time that morning. Probably time to swap over now.

"Right kids, I'm going to see Hayley. Stick together Ok?"

"Ok Mum." Panted Amy

"Ok Louise." Said Sam.

They were both a little red in the face and definitely out of breath, they had been nonstop for about an hour now.
"On second thoughts, before you run off again can you both come to the table and have a drink first. Just sit for five minutes please."

Louise gathered them to their table, just near the toddler section, Hayley was bent over spinning Flynn round and round the pole while he looked up, his mouth open in happy awe at the colourful ceiling.

"Hey." Louise plopped herself down next to her "Want me to take over now?" Quickly noticing Lucy about to go down the little slide she had crawled over to.

"Oh well done Lucy!" Louise clapped, smiling and watching her go.

"She has done that about three times now!" Hayley exclaimed "Such a clever girl, I couldn't wait for you to see."

"Oh, that's brilliant." Louise sat and watched not getting involved in helping her climb up the small steps that she usually found a struggle.

"Sometimes it's best to sit back and just let them do it, it's how they learn and great for their independence skills eh and confidence too." Hayley kept spinning Flynn.

"Absolutely. Here let me, your arms must be tired mate." Louise pushed Hayley out of the way and carried on spinning Flynn.

"Sam and Amy have run off again." Hayley noticed.

"Have they? Oh well at least they sat for a minute and had a drink. They're doing so well in there today, no incidents to report." Louise told her.

"Good, let's hope it stays that way or I'll have to go and trip some kids up." Hayley winked.

"You would as well."

"Yeah, I would!"

They both laughed, Louise was glad she had found socks with no holes in today, but the knees of her jeans were beginning to wear away she was always crawling round after the kids it literally wore her jeans out. These were definitely soft play jeans, the black long-sleeved t-shirt top clung to her slim waist, she sat cross legged now, positioned so she could watch Lucy repeat her climb up the steps over to the slide again, she didn't interrupt but smiled proudly knowing how long it had taken for this to happen while she spun Flynn round and round, him laughing happily at the feeling.

Hayley looked fresh and happy, she wore blue jeans with a silver belt, a bold red top coming to just past the top of her arms. Her curls tumbling everywhere.

"Stevie! Stevie!" A frantic Mum rushed past the toddler area holding a baby, eyes darting back and forth "Stevie!"

"Man, I hate that feeling." Hayley sympathised, watching the woman become a little more frantic.

"Me too." Louise agreed "So how was the rest of your week?"

"It got better." Hayley smiled wryly "Well it couldn't get much worse could it. Thanks for listening to me."

"That's what I'm here for." Louise smiled at her friend.

"It's just, do you ever feel that you wish you were…" Hayley couldn't seem to find the right words, "I love Flynn with everything I've got, he's my world but I just wish my son would look at me." Hayley's eyes suddenly brimmed with tears "And then I feel guilty because I feel like I want to change him and I don't want to change *him,* but I *would* change having to change his nappy 6 times a day or wipe shit off the walls, my flat smelling of shit, of him demanding food constantly but never actually connecting with me. I feel like a carer to him and not a mum. If someone else walked in and met his needs he just wouldn't care."

"That's not true mate." Louise stopped spinning to put her hand on her friend's arm.

"It is. That's what it feels like."

"No-one else could look after your boys the way you do, and Flynn does love you he just doesn't express it the typical way. He loves your voice when you talk to him in that tone, how you make bath time his favourite time of day, you know everything he likes and doesn't like and exactly how he likes it too."

"I know I know; I just need something back from him from time to time. With Sam he will come in and hug me or sneak in my bed and I don't kick him out, we will play games and laugh, he tells me he loves me, and I don't get any of that from Flynn, like it's just take, take, take." Hayley looked at him fondly and watched as he bum shuffled over to the steps of the slide, Flynn couldn't use his left side much at all, but he was strong and managed to get himself up, laughing as he reached the top of the slide, his mouth open in a smile as he slid down.

"Wow Flynn well done!"

"I feel guilty for even thinking those things you know. How much easier life would be if he was at least potty trained. Or if he came and hugged me once in a while, I would feel loved by him."

"He loves you; he can't show it the standard way, but he does love you. He doesn't tolerate anyone else in his room does he and does come and eat with you if Sam has finished. When he plays with your hair." Louise pointed out.

"Yeah, that does melt my heart when he does that." Hayley admitted watching Flynn climb the steps once more with Lucy.

"You know, as much as we love them, kids are selfish because they're kids. They don't realise were not super mum. Amy literally thinks I can do anything and as much as that puts a lot of pressure on me, I quite like it and Lucy and Flynn are no different in that way but it's the communication isn't it that's what's hard."

"Exactly! Communication! I mean he does communicate in different ways; he has different sounds for things, and I can just tell when he is upset or needs to leave, he is a happy boy though, I mean look at him."

Flynn was laughing again as he pulled himself up the steps towards the slide.

"He sure is mate and that's because you are a great mum, you make his life a happy one."

"Thanks babe. Sometimes you just need to hear it don't you."

Flynn slid down the slide again, landing at the bottom, his mouth open in a silent laugh. He made his way over to Hayley, pulling himself with one arm until he was close enough to be able to get on her lap, he sat there looking up at the bright lights near the ceiling and reached out to feel her hair.

"Oh Flynn." Hayley wanted to wrap her arms round him right then but that would have made him get off so instead she enjoyed this moment, this was him being affectionate and she relished in it.

"You know how to pull it out the bag for me don't you." She kissed the top of his head quickly, hoping he wouldn't pull away. He didn't.

"You know, I think It may be time for McDonalds" Louise said then as she checked the time. I'll go round up the other two, will take me a few minutes anyway."

"Ok mate." I'll sort these two out and get them in their buggies.

It had been a good day, the week was full of ups and downs as it always was but Louise's Saturday meet ups with Hayley and the boys always perked her up, gave her the much-needed injection of fun to push her on and the outlet of talking through the disasters of the week and triumphs too that she didn't get to share with anyone else at the end of the day really helped and Hayley just got it. She understood. She honestly didn't know what she would do without her, and she put the girls to bed feeling happy that they were alright. They struggled sometimes, money was a little tight, nothing ever ran smooth, and her home was never ever clean and tidy anymore no matter how hard she tried, but they were ok. She had her family and her friends that reminded her that sometimes it was ok not to be ok.

"You know." Hayley began as they were putting the kids in the car after their McDonald's earlier "We could do with a bit of girl time, no kids. How about a night out?"

Louise didn't hesitate "That sounds like a very good plan to me. I think we deserve it."

"Oh, we do babe! When are the girls next at their dads?"

"Next weekend actually, would your folks have the boys overnight?" Louise asked.

"I'm sure they would, I don't usually ask so I don't think they would mind."

"Ok great!" Louise was excited it had been a long time since they had been out. "You know what, I don't care where we go but I want to dance, I haven't danced in ages!"

"Cool. That's what we'll do... but watch out! After a few drinks you KNOW I am Kylie Minogue!"

They burst out laughing remembering the last time they had been out... Hayley really did think she was Kylie Minogue, inhibitions thrown to the side, strutting onto the dance floor like she owned it.

"Shame you can't sing like her. We'd never worry about money again" Louise winked.

"I can hold a note!" Hayley protested laughing.

"Hmmmm, a five-pound note at the bar maybe."

"Shut it! Right, that's it, I'll text you later babe after I have asked my folks yeah?"

"Ok, talk to you later Hun, thanks for a lovely day. Bye boys!"

"Bye girls!"

The friends had parted, happy with their plans, feeling lucky they had each other.

CHAPTER NINE

Louise's uplifted mood was long forgotten while she sat in the dreary hospital opticians waiting room. This was truly one of the worst appointments they had to endure. The room was a dirty yellow colour, drab looking which would ultimately match your mood after 45 minutes of running round, chasing the kids in the waiting room, trying to entertain them and keep the light happy go lucky mum voice, maintaining the pretence that you were as relaxed as you appeared even though the kids had begun to whine, you were getting irritated and running out of ideas not to mention energy. It was 11:45 and Louise was already thinking a glass of wine sounded good right about now.

Lucy's appointment was running 30 minutes late. They were always late here because kids hated the eye drops so all you could hear were the cries, screams and protests from the closed room while the nurses tried to entice the children to listen and have their drops without too much fuss.

Louise sighed in relief as Lucy stopped trying to hand out leaflets to everyone in the room and finally sat down in her buggy to eat some crisps when she noticed Jenny sat opposite her, seeming to be lost in her own thoughts while Paul and Mia sat together sharing a book. As usual they all seemed perfectly put together making Louise smile at her own comparison of herself.

"Hey." Louise moved closer a few seats, bringing Lucy with her in the buggy, noticing the chocolate button stains on the fabric and wishing she had seen them this morning before they left the house.

Jenny looked up in surprise. She was immaculately made up, her gorgeous locks looking like she had stepped right out of the hairdresser, her navy trousers and white fitted shirt more suiting an office job than a morning at the hospital waiting for hours on end for the appointment that seemed it would never come.

Louise could see Jenny trying to place her while she searched her face.

"Louise." She offered "I'm Lucy and Amy's mum. We met at one of the support groups earlier in the year."

Jenny's look flickered towards Lucy and back at Louise again, a look of recognition lighting her face.

"Of course! Sorry." She shook her head "I was in a bit of a world of my own there."

"Oh, don't apologise, happens to me often." Louise chuckled "Kids look great. How are they getting along in school now?"

"Oh, it's early days isn't it. Very different from nursery though." Jenny's brow furrowed slightly.

"Yes, it is." Louise agreed nodding "Especially with a whole different group of friends for them to get used to as well, not to mention us too."

"How do you mean?" Jenny asked.

"Well, we have to get used to the teachers don't we, how to connect with them so we feel better when we leave, the different mums at the gate, It's a massive change. But sometimes the kids are more resilient than we are."

Jenny laughed in agreement "That's so true!" For the first time, Louise had seen her smile without the cloudy look she had in her eyes. They had only met a handful of times before, but Louise had picked up on a wariness from her, a protective distance she put in front of people.

"What time is your appointment?" Louise asked.

"35 minutes ago," Jenny answered wryly. "I don't even think they need glasses to be honest, but their paediatrician wanted them to come so here we are."

"Oh, this is a regular one for us, at least twice a year. Once we were here so long that Lucy fell asleep, and they checked her eyes while she was sleeping." Louise rooted around in Lucy's bag for her drink and a baby wipe to clean away the crisp crumbs on her cheeks.

"Can they do that?!" Jenny was shocked.

"Apparently so. I was so stressed." Louise sat back remembering "I think I left here in tears. Had both of them with me, hours of whining. It was awful."

Jenny's kids lost interest in their book, approached Lucy in her buggy and started playing. They high fived and said hi then the boy picked up the book again to show Lucy. Louise and Jenny watched them smiling.

"That's nice," Jenny said quietly. "they find it hard to make friends."

Louise nodded in agreement "Yeah, same for Lucy. My heart always breaks when she goes up to another child to play and they just stare at her and ask their mum or dad what she is saying then walk away. I just keep to a select group now and try and keep her as occupied as I can when we're out."

"I noticed the bag of toys on the back of the buggy." Jenny smiled "You're prepared."

The kids were laughing now at a picture in the book and signing the first letter of their names; Jenny and Louise shared a look of happiness between two tired parents constantly worried their child wouldn't make friends, then watching it happen organically.

"That's nice." Jenny's face relaxed into a natural smile. She looked so much younger when she did that and Louise saw another side to her, a vulnerable side. "Lucy has your smile."

"Yeah gappy!" Louise joked, "We've all got it, me and the girls." Louise gestured to the gap between her two front teeth.

"Ha! That's not what I meant." Jenny laughed, then after a moment's thought she said, "We can all wiggle our ears." then showed Louise and Lucy "Look."

Jenny sat still and wiggled her ears, Paul and Mia seeing their Mum's party trick joined in, Louise tried to do it and kept making strange faces while concentrating and Lucy pinched her ears in between her fingers and shook them. This made them all laugh and didn't hear the optician calling out Lucy's name at first.

"Oh, that's us!" Louise said jumping up and waving at the optician, so she didn't disappear and call someone else instead. "Was lovely seeing you again Jenny, maybe we can meet up one weekend with the kids for a playdate." Jenny began to hesitate then watched her children waving and smiling at Lucy, happy to have made a friend.

"That would be lovely." She answered truthfully.

"Great. I'll send you a message, hope you don't wait too long. Bye kids!" Louise manoeuvred the buggy around the chairs and other buggies and prams in the full waiting room relieved to finally get called in.

The appointment in itself was only ten minutes long which always left Louise wondering how on earth they always waited so long if they were so quick, and

Lucy wasn't always the easiest; she hated them peering into her eyes with all the different lenses but Louise had developed a few tricks to keep her focused throughout so they could get an accurate reading.

"She will need a new prescription." The optician finally said, leaning back in her squeaky chair.

"Oh ok, what has changed?" Louise was hoping for good news.

"Both eyes have worsened, and she will need stronger glasses." The optician said dispassionately writing out a prescription and tearing it off with a practiced hand. "Here." She handed it to Louise "We will send you an appointment to check the eyesight in 6 month's time."

"*The* eyesight?" Louise was pissed off now. Lucy was a person not a thing.

The optician looked at Louise for the first time since they had walked in the door and had the grace to appear a little sheepish "Sorry. Her eyesight."

Louise gave the woman no more time and stood up, opening the door and holding it with her foot so she could pull Lucy's buggy out backwards while the optician watched her go not bothering to help.

Her foot falls echoed down the long corridor as she reached reception where the smiley woman sat who was always so nice; letting Lucy bang on the bell even when she was there and didn't need to.

"Bye ladies." She called and Louise smiled at her waving goodbye. They saw so many doctors, nurses, paediatricians, occupational therapists, speech therapists, cardiologists, physio therapists... the list seemed endless that she felt she was on a factory belt with Lucy as their job. Some were dispassionate, some lovely and kind and made the effort to connect with them both, but a lot of the time they all spoke like she was a thing not a person and would refer to *the* leg rather than her leg like it was something they were assessing and not someone. It riled Louise so much and by the time she got to the car she realised she didn't even know the optician's name.

But a good thing had come out of it, she had met Jenny and the kids today again, the kids had got on and it felt right to organise a playdate now. She smiled at Lucy as she settled her in to the car, clipping her up in her seat.

"We made some new friends today didn't we."

Lucy smiled and held her own hands, beginning to move them up and down signing "friends."

"Well done! That's it! Clever girl." Louise kissed her gorgeous plump cheeks before getting in the driver's seat.

"Ok let's go home." Relief filled her now the appointment was over, and she felt her neck muscles starting to relax again, it was always afterwards that she realised how tightly she was holding herself when she finally let it go. Louise did a final check in the mirror at Lucy and then glanced at herself before pulling away noticing the blob of toothpaste she had on her chin. On her chin! It had been there the entire time!

"I don't believe it! That's been there all morning, and nobody told me!" She laughed to herself and shook her head driving away.

CHAPTER TEN

Hayley gave an audible groan on the end of the phone while she listened to Louise's account of her morning; the phone balanced between her ear and chin, her hunched up shoulder having the job of cradling it while she washed the dishes. Hayley couldn't stand a messy kitchen; she was almost OCD with it, would recognise her anxiety building if the kitchen was in disarray and the boys began asking for food so religiously everything was packed away neat and tidily, usually with a Yankee candle burning away nicely on the windowsill, its sweet odour filling their flat.

"Not *Jenny Jones*!" She groaned again, this time taking the phone in her hands, tossing her tea towel over shoulder and leaning against the counter to give her friend her full attention.

"She is nice." Louise insisted, opening the fridge and reaching for the bottle of wine she had been thinking about all day. She would only have one she told herself; It was 7:30, the girls were asleep, and it had been a long day, plus after the eye appointment anyone deserved a glass of wine.

There was silence on the other end of the phone for a moment.

"Are you having a wine?" Louise could almost hear the smile in Hayley's voice.

"Just the one..." Louise smiled back.

"Ha! Well, it would be rude not to join you then I suppose!" Hayley opened the fridge pulling out her own bottle. "Where did you bump into her again?"

"The hospital for Lucy's eye appointment." Louise explained.

"Yuck! I hate those appointments! They take forever and it's so upsetting for Flynn, he hates them. No wonder you're having a wine."

Both friends were sat on their own sofas now, wine in hand ready to share their day.

"So, what did Jenny say?" Hayley wanted to know.

"Well, she didn't recognise me at first, she was in a bit of a world of her own. I had to remind her who I was."

Hayley harumphed on the other end of the phone.

"More like wasn't interested, I swear she is so far up her own-"

"I don't think she is you know." Louise interrupted thoughtfully. "I know why you haven't taken to her but there is something else, I think she's lonely."

"She winds me up Lou! I mean you click on Facebook and there she is with her perfect family, not a speck of dust or hair out place, everything so perfect it's like the cover of a bloody magazine! Every event perfectly documented with the right photo and caption, immaculately poised. The whole thing, she just doesn't seem..." Hayley searched for the right words.

"Happy." Louise said as the same time Hayley said.

"Real."

"Ahh" they both digested the other's description for a moment. Louise sipped at her wine "Maybe your right. Maybe it isn't real. I mean It is just a photo, but what's wrong if it is?"

"Because nobody is that perfect that's why and it just kind of makes me feel inadequate, I guess. But you could be right maybe she isn't happy." Hayley sighed. "Why do you have to be so nice to people?"

Louise grinned. "So, I can arrange the playdate?"

"Only because you're my best friend I will give her a chance, but I swear if she looks down her nose at me once..."

"I know I know you'll bite it off." Louise laughed. "It's just I remember how hard it was for me. Until we met."

The days before her friendship with Hayley had been dark ones; feeling so alone and isolated, Louise had never really had a lot of girly friends before; always concentrating on the job she was doing at the time and thrown into the relationship she was in, not much time for it really. She had friends, some really close ones but they were busy with work and she didn't like to complain but it hadn't been easy when Mark had left; she had wanted him to go of course, their relationship had been toxic together. When they had first met it was fun and laughter, long talks into the night, texting each other throughout the day, dinners out, evenings in; just them. Only them, like a protective bubble that could be so beautiful yet so fragile at the same time.

Mark never could share, and hated Louise's time being divided up once Lucy arrived; it had started in the pregnancy when she became tired and needed to rest more, instead of looking after her he became jealous and angry that she wasn't there for him in the same way, and this only got worse as time went on. She hadn't realised before how selfish he had become or how focused she was on being a parent, the rift between them becoming bigger each passing day when the realisation that the conversations between were only sharp, cutting comments, she would cry more than she laughed and was pregnant again, finding herself loving her unborn child so much already she couldn't bear to have it born under these circumstances and one evening while she sat crying after another argument when he had stormed out, it was decided they would separate. The relief had been immense, the air clearer and lighter straight away. Louise knew it was not going to be easy, but she did not want the girls growing up in a house of unspoken bitterness, chaos behind closed doors and a loveless tie between two people that clearly couldn't be together anymore.

Louise had learned to juggle everything alone, the appointments the tantrums, nursery, school, play dates, housework, cooking, holidays and she had chosen it that way. Mark would see the girls on weekends when his job would allow and that arrangement worked for them, but it had been hard on Louise emotionally, she had extra worries because of Lucy, things that her friends as much as they tried just didn't understand and Louise found herself going to a support group one day; the girls had been small, both under two and she remembered walking through the door at the Sunshine Centre (a place for disabled children and their families) for the first time, a lump in her throat which had been there permanently for months now before she decided to come and actually walk through the door.

She found a circle of women sitting haphazardly on the padded colourful floor, relaxed with a cup of tea, children of varying ages under 5 playing or in their Mothers arms talking amongst themselves. The room was filled with things you would find in a child's dream; a sensory room, a sand area, a foam table, book corner with hundreds of books displayed alluringly with a mat so sit on and teddies to cuddle while you read, dollies and dress up, kitchen with play food, cars and building blocks, paper, pens, an easel, paint with aprons so no one got *too* messy and this was before her gaze travelled to the open sliding doors leading out to the garden with slides, a sunken trampoline, the circle thing that went round and round but Louise never knew the name of, trikes of all sizes and adapted ones, a giant seesaw for disabled children. It was incredible and the light poured in from the windows giving it credit to its name.

This was where Louise found her safe place, where she could talk, where she found out she was not the only one who got a metallic taste in her mouth when she was becoming stressed or that she wanted to cry most days even though her children gave her great joy. She had met Hayley before briefly, but this is where their friendship blossomed and the Sunshine Centre was a place Louise learned it was ok to not be ok all of the time, that she did not have to be 'Super Mum'. After she got over her crippling fear of walking through the door, her insides shaking though her outward calm face and smile denied her true feelings, she learned to make friends that understood, and she felt much less alone.

Hayley sighed into the phone.

"I remember." She said, being taken back to the same memory.

"And she hasn't been in the area that long has she, it's not easy to start a fresh." Louise pointed out, not that she needed to; Hayley had already decided she would reach out and make an effort.

"Alright, you've persuaded me, but I mean what I say... If she annoys me..."

"I know! You'll bite her nose off." Louise laughed.

"Good. Glad that's settled. Now listen, I've got a question for you. What's good looking and hangs up?"

Louise clocked on too late and tried to hang up first but as always Hayley got in there first, it always made her laugh when she done that, and you could never tell when it would be. She texted her immediately calling her a bitch.

Hayley sent laughing emojis and Louise sat on the sofa smiling, feeling lucky and happy. Both girls had gone to bed ok after a good dinner, the appointment went Ok-ish and everyone was healthy today. She surveyed the room, toys were strewn across the floor, a couple of books still open and some washing needed folding on the dining table; it was an open living room, one part of it where the sofas were and the girls huge storage box that held all the toys, and the unit with the TV, Louise had separated the L shaped room with one sofa along one end so that the dining table behind it gave the impression of a different space, although really it was so she could keep an eye on them while she was in the kitchen and that they didn't stare at the telly too much while eating dinner.

The tidying up could wait, Louise poured another glass of wine and sat in silence, enjoying the peace and quiet.

CHAPTER ELEVEN

Louise closed the door softly after waving goodbye to the girls when they went off with their Dad, their bags and toys crammed into his blue Ford Fiesta. It made a rattly noise when it first started going... He really needed to get that sorted but insisted it was just because it was old.

Mark looked happy to see the girls and they had been excited too, they didn't often have sleepovers and had started it a few months ago now they were a little older and he had a bigger place too; It just made things a little better so they could have their own room, they weren't used to sharing a room but one night a fortnight made it exciting for them and they had been looking forward to it. Louise had rattled off instructions with Lucy's new medication she had been taking and the thickener she had to have in her drinks, she was always so worried he would forget something. Her anxiety irritated him, and he ended up scowling at her.

"Are you listening to me?" Louise felt herself becoming annoyed as she found him staring at her.

"No Lou, I know what to do. They are my kids too. Remember?" He growled.

The words stung. Of course, she remembered! But once a fortnight was not the same as every day and he could pick up the damn phone in between! He wasn't there for every appointment, slight change to medication, talks to the children when there had been night worries or something wrong at school, updates with the doctors. He needed to know, so of course he bloody well needed to listen!

"They're your kids *once* a fortnight" Louise smiled tightly as she closed the car door, making sure the girls didn't hear "There's a lot that happens in between."

"And whose fault is that?" Mark sneered at her and she wanted to slap his face.

"It's nobody's fault Mark it just is what it is." Louise sighed "Can you text me later when they're settled in bed please."

"If I get time." Was the gruff response.

Louise knew Mark hadn't wanted to split up years ago, but they weren't happy and that wasn't a good way to raise children, he always argued that apart wasn't a good way to raise children either. Truth was they would never agree on anything. Louise just wanted it to be a friendly and civil handover every two weeks and that way she didn't feel so sick with anxiety and worry each time she walked out with the girls to meet him knowing there would be some kind of showdown hissed quietly between them to avoid upsetting the girls. It was the smirks that riled Louise the most, those looks were the ones that really made her want to dent his head with something. But she composed herself, tore her eyes away from his; wondering what on earth she ever saw in him but forever grateful for the amazing people they had created together.

"Have a lovely time you three." Louise sang, blowing big kisses to the girls through the window. They waved enthusiastically back blowing kisses and smiling, Louise stood there waving until Mark had driven the car away, she knew he was throwing daggers at her in his eyes, but she held her smile knowing it would infuriate him all the more. My God she thought, who were the children here?!

The November chill in the air made her wrap her cardigan around her more tightly, breathing in the cool air. It was a fresh and sunny day and Louise had the best part of it left before she was meeting Hayley for their long-awaited girls' night out. Girls' night out! Wow it had been about 10 months since they had last done this, and Louise still didn't know what she was going to wear.

Louise: Hi! What are you wearing tonight? X.

Hayley: Hi! So excited! Don't know yet. It's between my new white blouse and jeans or I've got an old faithful X.

Louise: Wear the new one why not X.

Hayley: Ok. What about you Hun? Has dick head picked the kids up yet? X.

Louise: Yeah, just gone X.

Hayley: Did you argue? X.

Louise: As always! Looking forward to a drink later X.

Hayley: Me too, are you staying at mine tonight? X.

Louise: Is that ok? X.

Hayley: Of course. About 6? X.

Louise: Great, see you then X.

Louise was glad of the offer, she hated being indoors without the girls, it just didn't feel right. She spent a lot of her time needing some peace and quiet but when she did finally get that she actually didn't like it that much. Staying at Hayley's meant she could relax, and her mind wouldn't be going over and over what they girls were doing, if Mark had remembered the medicine and the correct dosage, if he read to them, if they went to sleep ok, if they woke up in the night and needed her. Would he ever tell her if they did? Probably not. Oh! But she needed the break too.

There was a mountain of paperwork to do, she hated paperwork she really did but there was so much of it and she had an afternoon of quiet now, so it was the best time to tackle it. Louise made herself a coffee and dumped the pile of letters, appointments, doctors' reports and school reports on the table along with the utility bills, bank statements and junk mail ready to sort through; file, throw away or pin on the calendar.

An hour and a half later and Louise was finished, back aching from bending over the different files. She had a file for Lucy and a file for Amy. Amy's file was thin in comparison to Lucy's. She had sections for everything; Opticians, Heart, Paediatricians, Physio, Speech, School, savings, Lycra clinic... the list went on. It helped her to be organised with Lucy's meetings once a year when they all got together, another one she hated because all the professionals would talk to each other about Lucy and not to Louise, her own Mother, because of course what did she know?! Over time Louise had begun to find her voice and demanded more respect but it was still daunting, the way they spoke about her as if it was a project for them. Louise guessed it was because they were desensitised, but it was insensitive, and she always started to feel uneasy about the meeting around a week or so before it was actually due to take place. The relief when it was over travelled down her back causing back ache after finally loosening the muscles she didn't realise she was holding so tightly.

"Right, that's done." Louise stretched her arms out standing up and looking at the clock, she still had four hours until she needed to be at Hayley's, what could she do? Louise inspected her nails closely, surprised how terrible they looked. She never usually had time to do them, or reason. Ok that was decided then, a soak in the bath, shave her legs, put on a face mask and do her nails so she would be completely relaxed for this evening.

The bath was bliss, she didn't have to get out to wipe a bum or have to lay there while singing nursery rhymes; she could also have it as hot as she liked with plenty of bubbles because no one was jumping in after her. Lucy hated bubbles, she would freak out if any touched her and it had to be much cooler for the girls, but Louise loved getting in the bath so hot she had to inch in slowly, it relaxed her muscles and she soon felt calm. Ten minutes later Louise was bored so after all her personal maintenance she couldn't soak any longer and decided to do her face mask and nails.

The afternoon slipped by quickly and soon she was putting on her make up and deciding on what clothes to wear, the familiar sensation of anxiousness began to creep up her chest.

"For Christ's sake it's just a night out." She said to herself committing to a black and white flowery slim fitting dress. This would go nice with her high boots she thought, but was it too dressy? Oh, sod it how many times in a year had she been out? Twice possibly. Louise pulled it over her head before she could argue with herself anymore refusing to look at herself in the mirror in case she found fault.

"Oh, Babe you look stunning!" Hayley exclaimed pulling her front door open wide, the smell of cinnamon spice wax melt escaping the flat.

"You sure? I wasn't too sure if it was too dressy? Oh, I love that top it really is you, you look beautiful." Louise said noticing Hayley's outfit.

Hayley had a bold red blouse, ruched down the middle with delicate black buttons shaped as flowers, her necklace was a silver chain with black flowers, and she wore black trousers.

"I haven't worn this for years and couldn't believe it when it fit!" Hayley looked really pleased with herself as she twirled around "Come on, let's have a glass of wine before we go."

"Smells gorgeous in here." Louise commented as she sat down.

"Yeah, I love those wax melts they really fill the room don't they."

Hayley's living room was inviting and comfortable, she was good at pulling different colours together to create an effect; she loved purples and cream with subtle shades of pink and the odd scattering of grey. Bold colours suited Hayley, just like the red she wore now.

The two friends raised their glasses in a cheers and sat back chatting about their day and as usual even when they weren't about, the kids.

"Can't believe he gave you grief again." Hayley said immediately sticking up for her best friend.

"Oh, I can, it's like second nature isn't it." Louise's thoughts went back to earlier, and she wondered what the girls were doing, if they had eaten properly, had a bath…

"Stop that." Hayley commanded.

"What?"

"That. Obsessing about the kids, they will be fine, they always are. Tonight, is our night off, let's enjoy ourselves." Hayley raised her glass.

"To our night off."

"Our night off." Louise countered.

Two hours later, Louise and Hayley were sat at Prezzo's tucking into a delicious meal each.

"This is heavenly." Hayley sighed dreamily, scooping more carbonara on to her fork.

"And we don't even have to wash up." Louise pointed out, enjoying every mouthful of her king prawn linguini, finishing off her glass of wine.

The restaurant was full, mostly of couples sitting together talking quietly, some tables had a family with the children creating more noise, dropping cutlery and crying occasionally but mostly it was couples and the odd table here and there who may be mother and daughter or friends getting together. Louise loved Prezzo's, the smells, the plants separating tables in the room, the food of course, even the wine glasses she loved. It was a real treat for them to have a meal out and they both enjoyed every minute of it.

"Corr have you seen that waiter?" Hayley said not so subtly, flicking her head to the side where he worked behind the bar.

"Oh, I saw him." Louise drooled "Probably a complete arsehole." She nodded as if confirming for herself.

"Oh absolutely!" Hayley agreed topping up both wine glasses "But we don't want him for his personality now do we." She sipped her wine "Just a now and again friendship would be nice." She winked.

"Now you're talking." Louise laughed "So where shall we go after this? Do I smell of garlic?"

An hour and a half later they were making their way up the steps to Las Iguanas dance floor and bar. The building was two floors, downstairs was a restaurant that served delicious food and upstairs a sort of nightclub but had tables and comfy chairs where you could sit, drink and chat until you were ready to hit the dance floor.

"What are you having?" Hayley made her way to the bar.

"Think it will have to be Disaronno and diet coke, I need the caffeine!"

"Don't flake on me now, the night is just getting started!" Hayley exclaimed.

The music pumped and pulsated through the room, songs they both knew and loved, before long they were dancing near the bar, enjoying the music, letting their hair down. It felt good, and as the dance floor filled up a little, the music became louder and they found their way on to the dance floor; inhibitions gone, singing at the top of their voices to each song.

Louise looked over at her friend Hayley and laughed; Kylie Minogue had made an appearance. There she was strutting her stuff and posing with each dance move, doing exaggerated winks and facial expressions as she moved about the dance floor. The bum wiggle was the best, Louise joined her and together they danced without a care in the world. It was exactly what they both had needed; Louise hadn't laughed like that in a long time. Two guys came over and danced with them for a while before they all ended up at the bar. The one interested in Louise was tall, probably over 6-foot, brown hair, nice smile.

"I'm Dave." He said introducing himself when they could actually hear each other.

"Louise."

Hayley and the other guy were chatting at the other end of the bar.

"Drink?" Dave asked signalling the barman.

"Yes please, Disaronno and diet coke would be great. Thank you."

Dave ordered their drinks and they talked for a while before Hayley came and dragged her back on the dance floor.

"I'll bring her back!" She promised Dave as they began dancing again "I love this tune!"

CHAPTER TWELVE

Louise's head hurt. Her feet hurt and she felt a little sick. Thankfully Hayley's sofa was comfortable, and she curled up hoping the feeling would pass.

"Morning babe." Hayley called groggily as she padded through to the kitchen barefoot.

"Tea?"

"Yes, please and tablets." Louise tried and failed to sit up. "Oh my God, I'm never drinking with you again."

"Please!" Hayley defended herself as she put Louise's tea down along with two paracetamol and some water "It was *YOUR* idea to do tequila shots!"

Louise sat up, gingerly reaching for the water and tablets.

"Fair enough." She admitted, tossing the tablets back and rinsing them back with the water.

They sat there quietly for a while, getting to grips with their hangover.

"Was a good night though wasn't it." Louise said.

"Yeah," Hayley grinned "Really great. I needed that, think we both did. To just be us for the night and not Mum."

"I know exactly what you mean. It felt good to dance like that too." Louise grimaced as she reached for her tea. "Doesn't feel so good now!"

They both laughed.

"Oh, those lads!" Hayley remembered "They were good fun."

"Yeah, Dave was it I think I was chatting to; he was nice." Louise tried to remember.

"He was good looking too." Hayley agreed "Mine got on my nerves after a while."

"They all get on your nerves. But he was nice though, he was really into you." Louise said "You gonna text him?"

"Nah" Hayley sipped her tea "I've had my fun, that will do me for another year or so. What about you? You gonna text Dave?"

"Don't think so, it's fun and everything but not reality is it?" Louise looked at her phone to check the time "Oh shit! Looks like I already have!"

Louise had given Dave her number last night, he had text her saying how happy he was to have met her and would love to take her on a date, she had only responded saying yes as well. Louise groaned as she looked through her phone.

"I can't believe that, why did I do that?" She moaned.

"He weren't bad babe. You should go on a date with him." Hayley suggested "You never know, you could really hit it off."

"Yeah, we could," Louise agreed "And then what? He will end up irritating me in some way or another and then there will be another messy break up. Standard." She sighed "There's no point."

"There's nothing wrong with going out for a meal and a good time with someone now and again mate, it doesn't have to lead to a serious relationship does it." Hayley pointed out.

Louise stood up picking up both empty teacups, feeling a little better.

"Very true mate. Very true. You gonna take your own advice?" She smiled sweetly as she went into the kitchen to make more tea.

"Fuckoff." Hayley called to her good naturedly.

Louise laughed and made more tea. She really had needed that night out, it had done her good to just be her for a change and not have to think about someone else, to just go out and have some fun, she felt better in herself even if her head was banging still. But at least she didn't feel sick anymore.

The girls were due back around 4 so she still had plenty of time to go home and tidy up, maybe get the ironing done too. She couldn't wait to see them, she really missed them this morning, missed seeing their sleepy faces when they first woke up and appreciated their soft hugs as she envisioned picking them up for their first cuddle of the day.

"What time are you picking boys up today?" Louise asked.

"About an hour." Hayley answered "Will take them out to the park I think, It's lovely and bright out there today.

It was a beautiful day, a chill in the air but sunny with just a few clouds and Louise wished her and the girls were going with them. The thought made her think of Jenny.

"So next weekend, play date with Jenny. What shall we do?"

Hayley thought for a moment "Well, as it's a first playdate and the weather is still good, I thought we could all meet at Thorndon Country Park. Its big enough so we all have plenty of space, and there's some lovely spots to have some lunch if we want to take a picnic. We won't be able to get away with that next month, it will be too cold and will start getting muddy, it's so hard to push their buggies in the mud isn't it."

"Sounds perfect," Louise smiled, "I'll text her today."

Louise drove home, happy but tired. Her dark circles under her eyes were a major tell tale sign as to her late-night last night. She sang along happily to the radio as she drove feeling lighter than she had in a while. It was good to get out and dance, despite the hangover she had felt like Louise for a while; not Mum or taxi driver, cook, clean, nurse maid and everything else in between. Just Louise knocking back a few drinks, having a dance and a laugh with her best friend, flirting with a guy. Oh, that guy! She must have been drunk to give him her number, knowing there was no point to it. He had been lovely though and made her laugh. Louise pondered for a moment, maybe she could go on a date, it was just a date after all. It didn't have to lead anywhere did it.

The thought of a man in their home, made Louise cringe. Being a single parent wasn't easy and some of her friends thought she should get herself a man to make life easier for her, but they were her kids and nobody else's. What if she was with someone for a while and they thought it would be ok to discipline them in anyway, would she be ok with that? Absolutely not. What if the girls got very attached to them and then things didn't work out so they would have to leave, that would be awful and hard for them to understand.

No, it was too complicated to even think about getting into anything with anybody right now, they had their own way of doing things, had their own groove and it worked. Louise would ignore the text and block him if she had to.

She went through the house cleaning with renewed vigour, spending extra time on the girl's bedrooms as they weren't there it was easier to organise. They had pink fluffy carpets, cream walls with different pictures placed on them, white furniture and a rainbow of assorted teddies, toys and games. Louise stood leaning against the doorframe smiling at the memories from this bedroom over the years. When they were babies, they shared this room but as they got older, they needed their own space. She used to get the sensory lights out and lay them across the floor after bath time, playing soft music and letting them explore the fibre optic lights in the dark. There had been so many memories of just them together, even when she was tired and it was the "Witching hour" Louise called it while they were toddlers; at a certain point in the day, it didn't matter what you did or how they just moaned and moaned. But after bath time they would chill out with the lights and books and cuddles. It was lovely.

Hearing a bib outside, Louise was shocked to find it was 3:35, it was too early to be them, but just in case she'd take a look. She slipped on some trainers, making her way to the carpark surprised to find Mark's car parked across the entrance to the alleyway already loading his arms up with their bags from the boot.

"Hi. You're early, everything ok?" She asked approaching the car.

"Yep." Mark clipped tightly, tossing the bags to Louise "Here you go."

"Did you all have a nice time?" She asked, meaning the girls but it was more polite that way.

"We had a lovely time." He straightened up, lips set in a thin line, she knew that's all she would get out of him and it irked her. Lucy couldn't communicate much so it was important they shared a conversation, even pleasantries about the weekend but he was acting childish again, she sighed not having the energy to argue and opened the back door.

"Hi girls!" She sang as a waft of sweet perfume hit her, confusing her at first until she noticed the blonde sitting in the front seat looking a little nervous.

"Hello." The blonde woman offered meekly. She was fully made up, hair perfectly styled, swept into a side parting. Louise could never stand those, they always got in her way while she was buzzing about all the time, but she liked the look of them, in fact she liked the look of her outfit, the jade green trouser suit and deep red high heels, but couldn't see why she would be wearing them this time of day unless they were going somewhere nice and why was she even here? Who was she?

The realisation that Mark had squeezed in his date before dropping the girls off made her sick, this woman around her kids! It hadn't even been discussed. Louise ignored her greeting and withdrew from the car slowly, turning to face Mark who at least had the grace to look away sheepishly. She noticed he wasn't wearing his usual tattered jogging bottoms and vest but an ironed pair of jeans and a shirt.

Amy flew into Louise's legs.

"Mummy! I missed you!" Then she ran for a hug from Mark "Daddy, when will we see you again?" She asked snuggling into his chest as he picked her up, a smile finally forming on his face.

Louise tried to keep her face neutral and helped Lucy out of the car, kissing her and saying hello.

"I'm going to need a hand to the door with the bags." Louise told Mark and began walking with Lucy, throwing one of the bags over her shoulder. She didn't need a hand, she was completely capable, had managed thousands of times before but she had something to say and wasn't going to do it in front of the blonde.

Mark half snorted under his breath and began to follow her with Amy still in his arms.

They were at the front gate when Louise finally turned to him.

"Once a fortnight you have them." Louise began "Once a fortnight and you couldn't wait to begin your little date, so you kick the kids out early to pick her up. Introducing *MY* girls to some stranger without even talking to me about it first." Louise threw the words at him, gone was the pretence that she wasn't bothered, she couldn't hold this in any longer.

"That's why you're early. Because your date was more important." Louise concluded.

"That's not it. I'm early because I needed petrol so I left earlier and the traffic was quicker than I thought it would be so didn't take me as long." Mark stood there, smirking at her. She hated him right now, how dare he do this without even discussing it first.

"Mummy I like Stacey." Amy announced, then turned back to Mark "I want to see Stacey again." She began in a whine.

"Next time." Mark told her, kissing her on the cheek and setting her down "I've got to go."

"Nooo." Amy held tightly to his legs and Louise told herself it wasn't personal; it was always like this when they come home after seeing him. Once a fortnight was not often and they missed him. It was easy to be a 24-hour children's entertainer, never saying no and indulging every whim when it was occasional. That wasn't parenting that was making life easy for yourself Louise thought darkly as she saw his smirk spread across his face again.

"Girls can you go inside while I talk to Daddy please?"

Louise helped Lucy up the step, then turned to face him again.

"You should have said." She hissed at him. "That was wrong. I don't want my kids around some tart you're sleeping with. Can't you keep your dick in your pants until they've gone home?"

"She's not some tart!" Mark defended her "We're living together."

The words floored Louise like a punch to the stomach. Living together? How long had this been going on for? When was he going to tell her?

"It's none of your business Lou."

"*It is my business.*" She couldn't help the rising anger spilling out into her mouth now.

"What my kids do, who they see and spend time is my business and you should have talked about it with me." She insisted.

Mark stepped closer, Louise noticed he smelled good and realised she was wearing her cleaning clothes looking hungover.

"They are my kids too." He said quietly "And I don't think for one minute, every time you go out and hook up with some guy, you think to run it past me, do you?"

"Hook up with a guy?" Louise laughed at the idea that she went out often and hooked up with anyone. "I'm home with the kids if you hadn't noticed."

"Until they stay at mine."

"Don't start acting like the doting dad, the sleepovers have only just started the last couple of months. They are 5 and 6! What do you think I've been doing for 5 years?!"

"You tell me." Mark raised an eyebrow.

They were interrupted by something falling over and Louise shot inside. She found the photo album on the floor. Louise picked it up in relief that it was only the photo album and not a vase or something else they could have hurt themselves with, berating herself for giving in to the argument and leaving the girls for a few minutes, she turned around to go and pick up their bags from outside the front door and Mark had gone; hadn't even waited around to see what the noise was. No of course he didn't, he had a date. Bastard.

CHAPTER THIRTEEN

Jenny sat in the car not wanting to be too early but not wanting to be late either, she tried to steady her breathing and concentrate on the papers filed neatly in her folder on the passenger seat, racking her brain of any more questions or points she wanted to raise instead of giving attention to the gremlin on her chest. He'd been there all morning, clinging to her, making her feel heavy, slowing her breathing and questioning every little thing she did. He told her negative things and made her heart pulse quickly, her whole body turning to lead as he sucked the energy from her.

Jenny slowly checked the documents again, concentrating hard on them; there was a lot there, she expected the meeting to be a few hours so they could update the kids EHCP, lots of professionals would be there too, all discussing their life. She trembled as she tried to wind the window down for some fresh air and sickness overcame her. Oh my god I can't be sick now! But she was and Jenny fumbled round for anything that would catch it, there was nothing, her car was pristine and nothing lying around there that shouldn't be.

In desperation she opened her door vomiting on to the floor, retching so hard it hurt her stomach, she didn't even have time to check nobody could see her. Twice more she vomited until there was nothing left, she was between two parked cars so hopefully no one would see her, and it was school time so no parents in and out right now.

Jenny sat back, shaking. Time check, she had to go now, or she would be late, mustering up her strength she picked up her papers again with a trembling hand, stepping out of the car over the splatter of vomit on the floor, the gremlin heavy on her chest. Straightening her shoulders, she walked towards the school for the meeting, blinking her tears away and cementing her smile in place, smoothing down her skirt ready to face everyone.

The room was full of people before Jenny got there, she recognised most of them but not all.

There was Mrs Mally, the kid's teacher, John Thread the Occupational Therapist, Susan Watts the Speech Therapist, Faye Hickman the social worker, the school receptionist, Jane Selway the Physiotherapist and someone Jenny didn't recognise. She made a mental note of all their names, pulling out a chair to settle down.

Jenny was the picture of calm, sat cross legged at the table, her white blouse tucked into a pastel blue skirt. She looked lovely. Her blonde hair twisted into a clip at the back, enough make up to hide her sleepless nights but not enough to be overdone, she looked more like a professional than a parent and said her hello's by nodding at those already there, she didn't quite trust her stomach just yet. Jenny organised her papers in front of her and bought out her notepad, she liked to write it all down, the things she needed to check back on, she didn't like to leave it to chance or to trust that the receptionist taking notes would remember everything.

"I think we are just waiting for Mrs Braith to arrive then we can begin." Mrs Mally said organising her own sheet of papers in front of her.

"I don't recognise that name?" Jenny enquired politely.

"Mrs Braith is the autism specialist." Mrs Mally explained.

"Autism specialist." Jenny repeated.

"Yes." Mrs Mally said

"Paul and Mia aren't diagnosed with autism." Jenny said an edge to her tone now.

"Yes, I'm aware, but we are very fortunate to have her visit our school and work with some children that have benefitted greatly from her help and input so have asked her to do some assessments. Anyway, we will discuss it all as we start the meeting." Mrs Mally was keen to break away from the icy glare from Jenny now, a palpable silence in the room as Jenny sucked her breath in. This hadn't been discussed previous to the meeting and there was no reason it shouldn't have been, it was exactly what made Jenny so anxious in the first place, the very fact they felt they didn't need to share important information with her, she was only their Mother after all! She felt unprepared now and not in control. Other people making assumptions and decisions on her own children.

At this moment, a short, plump woman wearing a deep purple dress, a red scarf and lots of bangles on her wrist entered the room, seemingly out of breath but smiling as she sat down. She looked at each person in turn saying hello, her face open and friendly. Despite herself Jenny warmed to her slightly.

"You must be Jenny, Paul and Mia's Mum. I'm Sophie Braith." She said, leaning across the table to shake her hand.

Jenny relaxed a little more towards her, firstly she had used her name and not called her Mum which almost all of the time the professionals did because they couldn't remember it which she understood, they must see a lot of parents each day, but it was much more personal for somebody to use your name and Jenny appreciated that. She also used the kid's names too, recognising them as individuals, instead of calling them the twins. She decided she liked this woman, but her guard was still up, she hadn't heard what she had to say yet.

The introductions began around the table; Jenny finding out that the person she didn't recognise was a new lady from the council called Mrs Unatawande. Mrs Mally asked for the updated 'all about me' to be distributed to each person so they could read it and they made a start. The professionals started with Paul's plan going through each section of what needed changing, removing or adding, Jenny had her own goals she wanted added to the paperwork and was insistent on them, she ticked off each item on her notes as she discussed them but was also keen to hear from Sophie Braith the autism specialist and sat patiently while it was her turn to add her piece to the conversation.

"Well, firstly thank you for inviting me today." She began. She had a soft woolly voice, kind of reassuring and Jenny correctly guessed kids would take to her quite well.

"I have had the pleasure of spending some time with Paul and Mia and I must say they are lovely, lovely children. Very kind and thoughtful." Sophie Braith said pointedly to Jenny who nodded in acknowledgement.

"I have completed some assessments and in my professional opinion I feel they could both benefit from some attention in autism sessions. These sessions are designed to increase their attention through specific activities. As well as increasing attention it also helps with gross motor skills and fine motor skills dependent on the activity, now I do know that Paul and Mia have not been officially diagnosed with autism, but they are however showing traits of being on the autistic spectrum and it is my opinion this should be investigated further so I am happy to write a supporting letter for the referral."

Jenny digested this and didn't think that she could disagree. Any help they needed she wanted wholeheartedly for them, but she wasn't happy about not being told of this development and decided to say so.

"Thank you, Mrs Braith." Jenny began, ever polite but ready to say her piece and turned her attention to Mrs Mally who seemed to anticipate this and steeled herself for Jenny's response.

"Whilst I appreciate all the support you have been providing for Paul and Mia, I do not understand why I was not made aware of this. If you feel Paul and Mia are on the autistic spectrum and this needs investigating, the first person who should have been informed was me." Jenny let her words fall on to Mrs Mally slowly before she continued. "I am their Mother and should have been informed and even asked of my opinion, this lack of communication is nothing short of insulting."

Mrs Mally was flustered, Jenny Jones always got her this way, she was so strong and formidable, never missed a beat and it intimidated her, she hadn't been sure of what she thought at first and wanted Mrs Braith's opinion before she said anything and as simple as that sounded in her head, getting those words out for her to understand seemed an insurmountable task right now as she watched the woman regarding her coldly.

"I -I thought it best to get my thoughts confirmed first before I bothered you with it." She attempted.

"I can assure you Mrs Mally, any contribution or thought to my children's welfare and education is never any *bother* of mine." Jenny was quick to say.

Mrs Mally found it hard to defend herself and simply nodded.

"So, who is making the referral?" Jenny wanted to know.

"Well now that we have the recommendation for referral from Mrs Braith and a letter of support then yourself or—"

"Ok I will contact the doctors and make an appointment or speak to the paediatrician." Jenny quickly took ownership of the task, writing a few things down of her own and asked for Mrs Braith's contact details, feeling some level of control return which calmed her a little.

The meeting continued for another hour and a half; Jenny's insides were like jelly by the time they had finished. Emotionally exhausted and drained from holding herself together so long against everyone had tired her more than she'd anticipated but at least she didn't feel sick anymore.

Mrs Mally breathed a huge sigh of relief once the meeting had ended, she had been dreading it if she was truthful. Mrs Jones was a tough cookie, she certainly seemed three steps ahead of everyone else and seemed to criticise with just a look. She was so efficient you automatically felt you had done something wrong in comparison, the twins were a lovely pair to have in class, loving and friendly and kind and she enjoyed working with them, helping them reach their goals but dealing with Jenny Jones was something that made her feel like she was the student and Jenny the teacher and she didn't like it, she felt Jenny didn't like any of them and wished she realised that they were all actually on her side.

CHAPTER FOURTEEN

Hayley listened to her friend, trying to make sense of what she was saying.

"Do you still have feelings for Mark? I thought that was dead and buried." She asked, flopping on to the sofa to get comfortable.

"No," Louise insisted, "I really don't. But seeing him today with someone, making an effort with how he's dressed, it was different and finding out they are *living* together! Well, he should have told me!"

"Yes, he definitely should have told you so you could have prepared the kids, that's just wrong. I mean he wouldn't like it would he." Hayley agreed. It wasn't often her friend got het up over things and she *was* annoyed, it wasn't like her "Are you *sure* you don't have any feelings for him?"

"I don't." Louise sighed. "I don't. It's just seeing him move on like that, as easy as that just makes me realise how I'm not and how easy it is for him to find that. Not that I'm complaining," She added quickly "Because I wouldn't change things for the world with the girls. Oh, I don't know, maybe I'm jealous." She confessed.

"I can understand that mate. He gets to be fun Dad every two weeks, everyone has an amazing time because It's now and then, It's not every day. It's not routine is it. Probably treats all day etc, no bed time and then she rocks up too and is different so it's a novelty for the kids and as long as they're getting attention and having fun they don't realise that he's not there all the time and you do all the boring stuff like making sure they have a balanced diet, going to appointments, cleaning up, school runs, play dates all that sort of thing; so you're the one actually being a parent and he's just having fun."

As usual Hayley hit the nail right on the head.

"Absolutely, and you know what I *want* the girls to have fun and be showered with attention while they're there, so they don't miss me." She paused "Oh I don't know It just hurt I suppose like they had all been playing happy families with the blonde."

"Go on that date." Hayley told Louise firmly.

"What?" Louise had forgotten all about the guy she had met on their night out.

"The guy. Dave. Go on a date, have fun, why shouldn't you! You are allowed you know."

Louise was quiet, she hadn't even returned his text, he probably thought she was really rude.

"Oh, I don't know."

"You should! Listen you can get your parents to have the girls overnight, they love having them and you can have a night out and bloody well enjoy yourself. You never know you may hit it off and if you don't, well then you had a night out."

Louise thought about it, maybe she would. Maybe. Her Father and Step-mum doted on the girls and always enjoyed having them to stay over, the girls enjoyed seeing their grandparents as well. It had been a little while since they had been...

"Anyway," Hayley broke into her thoughts "Talking of playdates have you organised Saturday with Jenny yet?"

"Were we talking about playdates?" Louise asked.

"I mentioned them about ten minutes ago, try to keep up. Have you sorted it?"

"Yes, I have messaged her, and we are meeting at Thorndon Country Park at 11. Is that ok?"

"Yes perfect. I'll meet you there. Text Dave." Hayley told Louise before hanging up.

Hayley smiled to herself after saying goodbye to her friend, she should go on the date, but she knew why she didn't. Knew what she was scared of; of liking him, maybe even falling in love with him and then of being let down which she knew her friend could cope with but what she would do anything to avoid is her children being let down if they got used to someone. Over the years Louise had dated occasionally but had always found an excuse to dump them, rather unceremoniously too for the most ridiculous of reasons as well.

"He stroked my thumb. *STROKED MY THUMB*!" Louise had exclaimed, curling her lip in disgust, "I mean what am I? A dog?!"

"He washed his hands, finger by finger. Took absolutely fucking ages to clean them and I was watching him thinking, honestly are you for real."

"He said the L word after three dates. Three dates!"

"Too skinny."

"Talked too much."

The excuses were endless.

Hayley laughed to herself, Louise was such a commitment-phobe and she didn't even realise it.

Hayley wasn't a commitment-phobe, she just didn't trust men. Period.

After Tim left, Hayley's world tipped upside down; heavily pregnant with Sam and caring for Flynn, still getting to grips with all his appointments and extra diagnosis that seemed to keep flying at her, and he left. She had never seen him since. They had not even had a conversation about it. Sam had not met his own Dad and she had struggled completely alone with it for 5 years.

She tried some parent groups at first, taking Flynn along while she was pregnant, trying to make friends to help keep her upbeat and sane but she never felt she fitted in. They were all so competitive and constantly talked about milestones. Flynn wasn't reaching any milestones yet, at 12 months old, he wasn't sitting unaided like the rest of their babies in the group which wasn't said as much but one woman did clearly say:

"Oh, Flynn isn't included in this conversation." Then dismissed them with a flick of a look before she turned to speak to the rest of the group, cutting Hayley and Flynn out of it like they didn't matter.

It hurt. It hurt so much and was so unexpected that the normally chatty, open and ready to tell you how it is Hayley was stunned into silence. She took Flynn home and never went back.

Face book was a friend and foe all at once; it connected her with all her friends, she was able to chat and laugh with them, play online games and felt part of a virtual world while she was stuck at home, but she had to endure the posts of the happy families; the doting fathers swinging their children around, laughing happily and looking with pride at his family, the updates of engagements, weddings and anniversary's. It broke a piece of her heart each time every day that she saw it, happy for her friends, yet sad for her children who it affected the most, growing up without even a memory of their father. Until instead of her heart being broken by it, she had learned to harden it, trusting no one, that way she couldn't be broken again, and no-one would ever do that to her boys. She protected them like a warrior, needing no man in her life, happy to just have fun and nothing else.

She felt alone though, all her friends that had children didn't understand Flynn's needs and didn't know what to say or avoided playdates because he wasn't interacting in the same way. There were a few people that still made the effort, but it was sporadic, and she needed more.

Finding the group at the Sunshine Centre had been the first step toward a much happier life, and friendship that she would never lose. That was where she made connections and felt she belonged, where she met Louise, where she found all the parents; mums and dads alike all helped each other and didn't compare regardless of their children's differences; they supported and lifted each other up. She found she could offload and laugh there, a light inside her grew and slowly but surely, she began to heal.

CHAPTER FIFTEEN

Hayley was right, Louise thought as she curled up on the sofa after tucking the girls to bed, reading to them and making sure they were asleep. She needed something too, something just for her. It was 7:45, she was sat alone on the sofa flicking through the channels of the TV with no intention of really watching anything, she sighed. It would be nice to have a date she thought, just a change of scenery from the constant cooking, running around for school drop off and pick ups, appointments, play dates, clearing up (not that it looked that way now after the girls had stormed through the building, all that was calm and clean before they arrived again was now in disarray and Louise did not have the energy to do it again).

Dates tended to make her anxious though, she would read far too much into everything, immediately comparing the situation in front of her while she was out to how it would affect the children at home. Would this person fit in her life? Did he have patience with children? Would he be responsible yet fun and sensible and everything she needed?

It was a lot to ask of anybody, but she couldn't accept any less and when she had met men that were anywhere near what she wanted it was all too real a possibility of them being close to being part of her life with the girls; she freaked out and found some reason to walk away. She knew this, it was what she did every now and again when she felt lonely and wanted to reach out to someone like she did now, she knew this even as she picked up the phone to text Dave, the familiar pattern of sparking up a relationship of sorts for a few weeks before it got too much for her trying to balance a personal life and care for the girls with her full attention as the man in question would become more involved and want more of her time. She just couldn't, she didn't have enough to give. Yet she did text him, knowing it wouldn't come to anything because she simply wouldn't let it.

CHAPTER SIXTEEN

They were graced with one of the few sunny and warmish days left before winter set in and Louise grinned as she pulled up at Thorndon Country park. Beautiful big trees surrounded the carpark and the visitors centre, magnificent thick, sturdy trees, their roots probably as deep as they were tall; their brittle leaves giving way to the autumn wind, falling to the ground delicately leaving an orangey brown carpet for the kids to kick in the air.

Amy sat forward smiling, she was looking forward to meeting her friends and Lucy began signing 'friends' with her hands. They drove through the 'tunnel of trees' Louise called it; where the road became dimmed by the shadows of huge trees either side, growing up and leaning into each other, letting slivers of the bright sun creep through.

"We're here girls! Time to see our friends." Louise said brightly, she was looking forward to seeing them.

'Friends' Amy copied signing with her, Louise smiled at them, they were so lovely together... sometimes. Earlier on that morning Lucy had hit Amy over the head with the lid of a saucepan but thankfully there was no lump and she had seemed to have forgotten that now.

She hopped out of the car checking she had everything on her list:

Picnic blanket, food, cutlery (you never knew) drinks, thickener for Lucy's drink, first aid kit (you never knew) change of clothes, Louise frowned at that and kept it in the back of the car knowing Hayley would take the piss. Baby wipes, tea towels, toilet roll, sanitiser...

"You know you're gonna have to carry all that."

Louise jumped as Hayley came up behind her, she could hear the laughter in her voice.

"What do you need all that for?!" She cried, leaning into the car, inspecting it for herself. Too late, she had seen the change of clothes.

"First aid kit, come on Lou, we're going on a picnic. Change of clothes!" She shrieked with laughter as Amy clambered out of the car wrapping her arms around Hayley's legs in a hello, Lucy waving her arms frantically and making excited sounds "Hi" She said over and over.

Louise helped Lucy out of the car and into her buggy now laden with so much it would surely tip over without her in it.

"You laugh now but remember when Sam fell headfirst into that pile of stinging nettles? We needed Calpol and calamine lotion and we didn't have either. Now we do!"

"Oh, I remember." Hayley grimaced at the memory.

"Hi boys!" Hayley had parked right next to her friend and Louise helped her get her bits out of the car, just the rucksack of picnic food.

"We travel light." She said with a wink and a pointed look in Louise's direction.

"I don't remember that Mum." Sam came over listening to the two friend's memory.

"I tell you what Sam, not that it was funny... but your mum..." Louise began.

"Oh, here we go!" Hayley threw her arms up and the kids smiled, they loved it when they all got together, their mums becoming animated, laughing and joking the way they did.

"Talk about dramatic! She picked you up Sam because you really did go headfirst into a big pile of stinging nettles, there were sore red lumps all over your face. She picked you up, trying to make you feel better and then declared..." Louise raised her arms up for effect, Hayley shaking her head knowing what was coming, "I'm gonna sting myself!"

They all laughed then; Lucy was happy just having fun. Flynn sat beside her in his buggy saying hello by letting her hold his hand for a few moments and Louise and Hayley looked at each other smiling.

"That was a stressful day." Hayley said still shaking her head.

"Certainly was mate." Louise agreed.

"Good morning." Came a cool measured voice. Both friends turned around to see Jenny standing there with Paul and Mia, all holding hands. They were certainly dressed for an outing in the woods; Paul and Mia had wellies and warm looking raincoats, both looking excited and began waving at Lucy and Amy, Sam and Flynn immediately. Jenny looked picture perfect with her blue jeans, walking boots (clean ones) a gorgeous lightweight khaki coat and a rucksack on her back, as usual her hair and make up done to perfection. She looked like a model. Louise could hear Hayley's thoughts as she made a mental note of her own dress wear; un-ironed jeans from yesterday with probably some remnants of last nights dinner on them, dirty old trainers that she used specifically for the woods and a coat she had pulled out the cupboard this morning, she loved it because of all the pockets, it made life easier with the kids constant need to give her items they found while out walking. Hayley was similarly casual, but Louise thought she pulled it off better, she always had decent tracksuits with nice trainers because she went to the gym or running which, she wore this morning, and her hair was done nice too.

"Morning." They both said in unison, genuinely pleased to see her though, despite feeling a little over shadowed. After a moments silence Louise suggested they head off.

"Have you had a good week Jenny?" Louise began making conversation while navigating Lucy's buggy over the bumps and tree roots taking over the path. She was sweating already now, wishing she had left the coat at the car.

"Yes, good thanks. Have you?" Came what seemed the automated response.

"Yeah, so so," She replied, "Up and down."

Hayley laughed as Paul and Mia tried to help Sam climb a tree, but he fell backwards into a pile of leaves, giggling happily.

"Ahh look at them, your two are so lovely Jenny." Hayley told her.

Jenny nodded, smiling, then stopping to take a picture. She stopped herself just before she did.

"Is it ok if I take a picture with your kids in it?" She asked suddenly unsure of herself.

"Of course it is, just be sure to send a copy to me too." Hayley told her.

"Sure." Louise said, huffing with the extra weight.

"You didn't need all that mate." Hayley said.

"Don't start with me. You know it could come in handy."

Jenny eyed the two friends unsure of their banter and they continued walking for a while watching the kids run off and play. Amy would come back and forth with pinecones, conkers, special looking stones and kept piling them in to Louise's pockets. Sam ran back and forth kicking up the leaves and Paul and Mia climbed trees. Flynn and Lucy were content for the time being pushed in their buggy's. They came across a flatter piece of ground with some logs they could use for sitting on and some good low tree branches, just asking to be climbed so they all decided this was a good place to stop for lunch.

"I'm hungreeee." Amy whined as soon as the word lunch was mentioned.

"Ok, let's set out the blanket then shall we?" Louise tried to locate the blanket as Lucy decided to unclip herself and climb out of the buggy, causing the back of it to tip backwards; the contents of the first aid kit strewn across the grass.

Louise groaned, Hayley laughed, and Jenny covered her eyes.

"I don't believe it!" Louise exclaimed as they all began helping to pick it all up.

"I do!" Hayley said, running after the sterile tape as it rolled away from them. "That was bound to happen."

After everything had been picked up and put away, Louise unrolled the blanket and called the girls over. Jenny did the same and Hayley plopped on to Louise's blanket.

"Sharing my blanket, now are we?"

"Of course! I don't want to sit on the mud." She grinned and shoved her friend playfully, they all pulled out their picnic sandwiches and treats, helping themselves to each other's like a buffet, sitting in companionable silence as they ate; the kids quiet for the first time since they had gotten there.

Amy had eaten quickly, eager to go and play and got up as soon as she could.

"Let's make a den." She called over her shoulder.

Paul and Mia hadn't finished yet, but the idea of a den was much more exciting than their lunch so got to their feet and ran off too, closely followed by Sam.

"Wait!" Jenny called, reaching for the baby wipes. They hadn't cleaned their hands yet she realised.

"Oh, they'll be fine." Hayley reassured her seeing the worried look on Jenny's face, "They will probably need them more on their way back!"

Not having the kids around to occupy her thoughts and seeing them doing just fine playing with the others, Jenny was at a loss with what to say or do but Hayley was good with putting people at ease and as she tore apart more sandwiches for Flynn, she chatted about food, Christmas gift ideas and what colour decorations she was going to put up this year. They were easy subjects to fall into and the three of them chatted for a while. Lucy finally finished enough food for Louise to let her have her crisps, she would eat crisps all day if Louise let her.

Jenny felt envious of the easy way the two friends talked and laughed; sharing snippets of memories they had collected over the last four years. The bond between them was strong and easy to see, despite the constant light-hearted bickering and mickey taking, as equally comfortable as the silence that arose from time to time when they would reflect on the children or what somebody had said; seeming to know one another's intentions and needs, naturally and instinctively helping out. She heard them talk honestly about their bad days and how they reassured each other, Jenny could relate but said nothing.

The time passed quickly, with Jenny listening to the conversation and joining in with a non-committal answer occasionally, whilst watching Paul and Mia play. It was nice to be out in the fresh air like this.

Jenny had never really shared that with anyone apart from Chris and the realisation of it hit her unexpectedly as she remembered times when she and him had picnicked alone together before the kids were born or driven around for hours just talking; sometimes curled up in front of the switched off TV, never running out of things to say to one another. They had been best friends a long time before they were ever lovers and she missed that. She missed having a friend. The feeling unsettled her so she pushed it away quickly, but the familiar heavy feeling had shown its presence and now it was here, she couldn't ignore it. Jenny began busying herself with the picnic bits. Sorting them out and packing them neatly away to be able to have something else to concentrate on.

Hayley and Louise noticed Jenny packing up.

"Oh, is that the time already?" Hayley made a point of looking at her watch.

"I'll round up the kids." Louise offered, getting up.

They made their way slowly back on to the path where it was easier to push the buggies, the November sun low in the clear sky, a chill creeping around their toes as the temperature dropped.

Paul, Mia, Sam and Amy ran alongside them, skipping and hopping, sometimes balancing on fallen logs; all in a line copying each other. It was fun to watch and made them all smile, Lucy laughed, and Flynn began to moan as his cheeks grew red with the cold. Sam jumped in front of the line, balancing his way across a tree root that got bigger in size and higher as it reached the trunk; his normally cautious nature put aside as he climbed the branch attempting to walk it tightrope style. They all saw him wobble.

"Sam!" Hayley called in fright as he fell off the branch.

Jenny was quick; she jumped forward catching him before he hit the ground.

"Oh Sam!" Hayley rushed forward, plucking him from Jenny's arms who was crying from the fear of falling not from actually being hurt. "You're ok, you're ok," She soothed him. "No bruises, no scratches, see?" She cuddled him for a moment, waiting for his tears to pass.

"Sam," Amy came and gave him a hug "You're so brave."

"You are Sam." Louise agreed. "But, let's all keep our feet on the ground now shall we."

"Yeah," Hayley nodded. "No more tree climbing for now eh."

She turned to Jenny, crisis over as the children carried on their game from before, tears forgotten.

"Thankyou!" She said whole heartedly. "He could have hurt himself if you hadn't caught him!"

Jenny smiled, "No problem." Then after a moment's pause, "It's a good job there were no stinging nettles around."

Hayley caught the glint in Jenny's eyes as she realised she was referring to the story they had been telling before and had clearly overheard. She was taking the piss! Jenny actually had a sense of humour!

Louise stopped and bent over the buggy laughing, not just at the joke but at Hayley's shocked face. Soon they were all laughing.

"Good job he didn't fall right to the ground really," Louise laughed, "I can just imagine the drama of you running up the branch and launching yourself off just to see how much it hurt!"

By the time they reached the carpark, they were cold, tired and happy. Louise would be taking home half the forest in her pockets, somebody had trodden in dog shit and Amy was dragging an enormous tree branch with her, refusing to listen to reason that it belonged in the woods and insisting it come home; but the near miss and the laughter that followed had somehow bonded the trio of mums.

"Was a lovely afternoon girls." Hayley said, wrapping her arms around Louise as she always did, then turning to do the same with Jenny , who became stiff in response but allowed the hug. "And thank you *both* for making inappropriate jokes about the well being of my son."

Jenny's jaw dropped and Louise nudged her.

"Oh, take no notice she's winding us up. Was lovely mate, text you later on."

The sun, dipping now along with the temperature, bodies warming up inside the car, letting the heater warm her toes before she started to drive, the tyres crunching slowly along the ground, jenny smiled, and not because anyone was watching, she just smiled.

CHAPTER SEVENTEEN

Hayley's week started well, she managed to get both boys to school Monday morning without any issue and took herself to the gym. Hayley loved the gym; this was *her* time. All the pent-up feelings, anxiety and stress she worked out forcefully with each step on the running machine and the rowing machine, concentrating on her movements, zoning out. The beat of the workout tunes throbbing in her ears, moving rhythmically until her muscles ached. It was cathartic. Here she didn't have to change nappies, wipe bums or read books, spoon feed, clean or cook or listen to teachers, doctors, arrange activities, be something for someone else. Here she was just Hayley and it felt good.

After a full hour of focusing on her workout, Hayley finally looked up and checked out the room. She wanted to try some muscle workouts today, wanting to build up some strength in her arms, but usually avoided the weights because of all the muscle men in that part of the gym, it was sort of intimidating. She was thinking about going over there and that's when she saw him. At first, she didn't even notice him but as she was scanning the room, Hayley became aware of someone staring at her. She tried to ignore it but did a double take when she realised it was the guy from the bar two weekends ago.

"Shit." She mumbled to herself, she had seen him now and he had seen she had seen him, there wasn't any getting out of it as he put down his weights, smiling and walked towards her.

"Hi." He said a little hesitantly, stopping just in front of her machine, maybe he could see she wasn't interested. She certainly hoped so.

"Hi!" Hayley injected a falseness into her voice.

"Haven't seen you down here before." He commented, looking a little uncomfortable now, seeing Hayley's unenthused reaction.

"Oh, I'm not usually here on Monday's." She explained. And I won't be coming again she thought to herself.

"Oh. Mondays is my day off so I always am here then, and usually in the evening when I can."

He shifted from foot to foot as Hayley took a drink from her water bottle.

"I'm Simon from the other night." He explained to break the silence.

"Yes, I remember," Hayley smiled, "It's nice to see you, just... unexpected that's all."

"Oh." Simon looked away and Hayley began to feel guilty.

"It's just that I'm not exactly looking my best!" She laughed and pretended to sniff her armpits.

Simon laughed too, sitting down on the rowing machine next to her.

Oh, fuck off! She thought. She was trying to be nice, and he has taken it as an invitation to sit down.

"Nonsense, you look great. Not the same as the other night, but you do look great." He smiled, causing crinkles round his eyes. He had nice eyes Hayley thought, she hadn't really noticed the other night when she had met him, maybe it had been too dark, or maybe she just hadn't bothered to look. They were blue grey, steely sort of she thought, realising she was staring.

"Um thanks." She looked away.

"I'm sorry," Simon stood up looking a bit sheepish "This is your gym time and I've completely interrupted you. I just saw you and wanted to say hi. It was lovely meeting you the other night and I didn't think I would get to see you again so when I did see you ..." Simon trailed off and Hayley watched as he shrugged then began to walk away.

He was quite unassuming really; unlike a lot of the guys she saw here. No fancy gym wear, just plain old black jogging bottoms and a black t-shirt. He had lovely hair too, not too short, light brown.

"No wait," Hayley called without thinking, Simon turned around "You just caught me off guard that's all."

The slow smile that lit up Simon's face softened Hayley a little and she found herself accepting an offer of coffee. She wouldn't be able to continue her work out now, anyway, having been distracted from her zone and had become too aware of the men beefing themselves up in the mirror in the side room where she had been wanting to go to do some free weights. It was off putting, if she hadn't been distracted, she would be in the right mindset. But Simon was not a bad distraction, certainly a nice-looking distraction she thought as she slipped her jeans on and sprayed some deodorant in the changing rooms. Hayley checked herself out in the mirror. Damn! Why didn't I bring some make up?

"Because I'm working out at the gym that's why."

She looked flushed from the workout, her jeans were nice slim fitting ones, and her black top was at least fitted, she looked ok, but it was just coffee and an impromptu one at that. The work out had caused her curls to tighten with the humidity. She tugged at them uselessly with her comb as they sprang back defiantly.

"Oh, what am I doing?" She groaned to herself.

A mental flashback of her telling Louise that not everything had to lead to a serious relationship popped into her head, making her smile to herself. She shook her head, maybe she should take her own advice!

Before Hayley could change her mind, she grabbed her handbag, knowing there was a lipstick in there. Bingo. She found it.

"In for a penny…" Hayley puckered up in the mirror, applied her lipstick; grabbed her gym bag and headed off to meet Simon for a coffee in the upstairs café before she could change her mind and leave him waiting (which she had considered doing).

It's just coffee, it's just coffee, she told herself taking the stairs but as she opened the glass doors to the café and saw him sitting there, his head spinning round at the sound of the open door expectantly, his blue grey eyes meeting hers, causing her heart to flip and mind race at the same time. She knew it was *not* just coffee.

Coffee turned in to lunch. Lunch turned in to more coffee and then it was time to do the school run. All Hayley's afternoon plans had gone out of the window. Thank fully she had no jobs on that day because of a cancellation. As she scrambled to the car leaving it as late as she could she cursed herself. She did not need this complication! Things were fine as they were. Simon's number on a napkin in the back pocket of her jeans nagged at her all the way to the school.

Dating was a pain in the arse when you had kids, you had to find a babysitter, couldn't talk on the phone when they were awake, couldn't have people over. By the time it was time to leave to go out for dinner you were already starving having been used to eat so early with the kids for so long. There was a long list, and then after a while, maybe a few weeks one of you would get bored so all that effort was a bloody waste of time anyway!

Hayley found herself daydreaming at the school gates, but it *had* felt nice to be talking to a guy that wasn't one of the kid's teachers or Flynn's doctors or physiotherapist, she had laughed and felt easy and relaxed with him, talking about their lives but keeping it light. No heavy stuff.

She had learnt he was 37, a little older than her. Had been married but divorced after he found her cheating but didn't expand; just shrugged it off although Hayley detected a trust issue there which she could relate to, didn't have children yet, he had been single a few years, and was a carpenter with his own business.

"Mum!" Sam flew into her legs "I got a merit today!" Sam thrust his achievement into Hayley's hands as she hugged him hello.

"Oh, wow that's amazing! I'm so proud of you!" Hayley read the award it was for his improvement in maths, he had really struggled with his timetables last week, so they had spent hours over the weekend going over them, learning rhymes to help him and writing them down, it had obviously made a big difference. Sam's smile melted her heart as they walked to the car, him chatting a mile a minute, Hayley trying to keep up; Simon's blue grey eyes fading to the background and the number on the napkin in her back pocket forgotten.

CHAPTER EIGHTEEN

Louise towel dried her hair, eyeing her wardrobe wondering what on earth to put on. Her stomach was in knots now and she had to keep going to the toilet. This always happened, damn, she would lose a stone by the time he picked her up.

Amy and Lucy were happily playing with the babysitter downstairs and she had an hour to get ready. The anxiety seemed to rise up not from her stomach to her chest causing her to get breathless.

Why oh why had she agreed to this? She knew where it would end up didn't she, just because Mark was clearly ready to move on didn't mean she was or even wanted to. She looked around her bedroom, it was her sanctuary; decorated in cream walls, white furniture and soft peach curtains, pastel green bedding on her lovely big double bed. Pictures of her and the girls placed around the room and one big painting of the woods in autumn, her favourite time of the year. She loved her bedroom, it was where she came to read, relax and have time to herself. There was the odd toy and pile of the girl's clothes in the corner waiting to be ironed (it would be waiting a long time) Louise thought with a wry smile. A Peppa pig bedtime story book on her bed side table for when the girls would climb into her bed after their baths to be read to before Louise put them in their own beds. It was lovely, just right for them. She tried to imagine men's clothes added to the pile of laundry to be ironed and shook her head. She didn't have room in her life for a man, she didn't or couldn't bring herself to add that facet to her life. It was good this way, simple but good. Hard sometimes juggling everything... ok, very hard but it was the way she knew.

Not too late to cancel she thought as she picked up the phone, but it had been a long time since she had been out and he was so nice, they had really hit it off. Perhaps she just hadn't met the right one yet that she would be willing to open up her world to. Perhaps she should stop thinking. Perhaps she should just get dressed!

Louise dried her hair, then straightened it, put on her make up slowly taking extra care this time with it than she did day to day, she decided on a woollen dress; it was grey and black, fitted until past her bum where it ruched out a little and then carried on, it was warm, sexy and she felt good in it. Black tights, boots, some silver jewellery and she was all set. She needed a small black clutch bag to go with it, damn it where was it?

"Oh no." Louise groaned remembering the girls playing with it when they were dressing up, practising with their make up. Louise found it at the bottom of the wardrobe covered in eyeshadow and what was left of a red lipstick squashed inside.

"Louise, there's a bib outside my lovely." Stef called. She had been the girl's babysitter for years, she was one of the few people Louise actually trusted with the girls.

"Ok, coming!" Louise grabbed a red handbag from inside the wardrobe and raced downstairs before he could get impatient and knock. She had told him not to knock, but you never knew.

"Bye girls, have a lovely time with Stef." She kissed them both; they were all clean from their bath, smelling fresh and snuggled in their warm fleece pyjamas watching Cbeebies on either side of Stef with a blanket. "Love you." She called on her way out the door. No time to be nervous now, no time for anything, he was here.

Louise saw his car and made her way over there. Soft music was playing and as she opened the door, she could already smell the aftershave, it was nice but pungent and she fixed a smile in place before climbing in.

"Hi." Louise said lightly, her demeanour showing a confident woman, happy and at ease. Not at all the nervous wreck that she felt inside.

"Hi. You look beautiful." Dave said leaning forward to kiss her on the cheek.

"Thank you, you look nice too." And he did, he wore a light blue shirt with black trousers, he did seem nervous.

"Are you hungry? The table is booked for half an hour, so we had better get going." Dave waited for Louise to clip her seatbelt in to place before driving off. His car was much cleaner than hers, smelt better too; after the wave of aftershave had died down a little with the help of Louise discreetly undoing the window a crack despite the cold air outside, she could notice the lemon air freshener attached to the middle air vent. There was literally no rubbish anywhere in the car, no sticky finger marks on the windows, no white chocolate stains on the upholstery, just a very clean and tidy car. Louise was very glad she hadn't offered to drive.

CHAPTER NINETEEN

Jenny lay there awake. Again. Chris's soft breathing, rhythmic and low. She lay there staring at the ceiling wanting to be tired, hoping to fall asleep; desperately fed up with this exhausting routine of never being able to switch off, going over every part of her day. She had enjoyed the play date with Hayley and Louise and all the kids and what's more important she knew Paul and Mia did. It was wonderful to see them making friends and not witnessing other people's children playing with them to be polite because their mums said so.

She had overheard one of the parents talking about them at the school gates once saying they belonged in a special school and were holding the other children up. This had kicked Jenny so hard she physically stopped in her tracks, her feet betraying her from walking up to the woman and giving her a piece of her mind, her throat closed in shock. So, she just stood there fighting back the tears until her legs began to walk again, taking her to their classroom ready to welcome them with open arms and the biggest smile she could find. After that she didn't bother anymore with the other parents, she wasn't particularly sociable anyway and that just cemented it for her. She wanted the kids to have friends and found it hard to arrange playdates not knowing who genuinely wanted to spend time with them or not.

Paul and Mia were gorgeous kids, so kind and thoughtful, they didn't always understand other's games if they were too quick or complicated so would walk off and play alone together, they always understood each other but didn't like too much noise either so if games became too excitable, they would slowly back away, when there were sudden loud noises Paul would run. He could run so fast too!

Friendship was important for them and Jenny wanted them to have friends. She didn't realise just how important it was until today when she saw them playing with kids that accepted them without question. If they didn't speak Sam and Amy were used to that and just signed instead or took their hands and run off with them to play, you didn't always need words. It was beautiful; it warmed Jenny's heart.

She had felt good being with them all if she was truthful, it made her ache for the kind of friendship Hayley and Louise had, so easy and strong.

Jenny looked over at Chris, wishing she hadn't pushed him away as much as she had. She literally had no idea how undo the damage she had caused and didn't know if she would be able to even if she knew how. Something stopped her every time. An invisible force between them like a pane of glass. She wondered if she could reach out and touch it. Would it feel cold and hard? Like the way she knew others saw her. Or would it bend? Would it wake him? Was it even there?

The love they had shared was a distant memory now, but still delicate and beautiful like a bubble with hints of colour as it shone in the light so precious you couldn't touch it, or it would disappear. Or would it burst? Or pop? Or would it shatter like glass? the memories becoming nothing more than broken shards scattering into nothingness.

Jenny's tears travelled silently down her cheeks. She never told Chris about the woman at the school gates or the moments she shared with Louise and Hayley, she kept it all inside. She simply said it had been a good day.

Chris worked hard, he needed a stress-free home life and Jenny would give him that, she could at least give him that after failing him the way she had.

Sleep was impossible. Jenny checked her phone 11:45, she was literally wide awake now, her brain showing no signs of stopping. Jenny slid out of bed as silently as she could and crept downstairs. The loudly ticking clock the only sound to be heard. She stood there for several minutes staring into space then made her way to the liquor cabinet, pulling out a bottle of red wine.

Chris found Jenny sleeping soundly next to him in the morning, unusual really. Usually, she would be up at the crack of dawn getting everything ready for the kids, planning their day and making breakfast. He could hear the kids stirring so as quietly as he could he crept out of bed and out of the room, taking care to close the door; excited to be able to see to the kids first for a change and make her a coffee in bed, maybe get the breakfast ready too. Chris tiptoed along the hall meeting a sleepy Paul coming out of his room.

"Hey buddy," he whispered. "Mummy's sleeping, let's wake your sister and go and make her a special breakfast, shall we?" Paul's sleepy eyes sprang open in excitement. This never happened! They never got to make a fuss of Mummy, she was always up and ready and they got to do it with Daddy too.

"Mia, Mia" Paul Whispered gently shaking his sister "Shhh." he said as soon as she opened her eyes.

"We're making Mummy breakfast." Chris told her.

Creeping downstairs, all three of them were excited to be spending time together and doing something special for Jenny. Chris herded them into the kitchen, closing the door softly.

"Right, shall we make pancakes?" He grinned knowing it was Paul and Mia's favourite too.

"Yes!" They cried together.

"Shhhhh!" Chris reminded them smiling, a finger pressed against his lips.

They set to work messing up the kitchen, making pancakes as quietly as they could. It was a real novelty for all of them and they had fun. Chris got fresh coffee ready to take up on a tray as the pancakes were sizzling away, when he noticed the empty wine bottle down by the side of the bin where they kept the recycling before taking it out. He was confused for a minute, she had gone to bed before him, he knew she wasn't asleep when he went to bed, she never was but they both pretended as they always did. This must mean she got up again when he was asleep. Sorrow replaced his excitement as he flipped the next pancake while the kids laughed and got their plates ready too.

No wonder she was still asleep. Chris got her tray ready adding a glass of water and two paracetamols to it, Mia ran off to take a flower from one of their vases to lay on the tray and Paul drizzled honey over her pancakes.

"Morning Mummy!" The kids clambered over her in bed, happy to be surprising her.

Jenny's eyes did not want to open but the sound of their voices brought her back to life. Oh goodness, what time was it?

Jenny sat up, the kids hugging her, her head splitting with the sudden movement. She noticed Chris standing at the foot of the bed holding a tray. She could smell coffee, oh she needed coffee!

"Morning." Chris said, smiling at her with fondness. Jenny felt disgusting, she certainly didn't deserve this kind of treatment.

"Breakfast!" Paul shouted as Jenny saw the pancakes too.

"You made me breakfast?" Jenny asked bewildered "What time is it?"

"Don't worry about that," Chris reassured her "We wanted you to be looked after for a change."

Paul and Mia wriggled off the bed and ran downstairs to eat their own pancakes, Chris let Jenny sit up properly, setting the tray down gently on her lap.

"I don't deserve this." Jenny said quietly looking at the beautiful tray, seeing the effort they had all gone to.

"Yes, you do." Chris told her firmly. He hesitated then kissed her forehead before leaving the room to see to the kids.

Jenny's head was banging now and as she reached for the coffee, she saw the two paracetamol sitting next to the small glass of water. He knew, she realised. He knew and he didn't even say anything.

CHAPTER TWENTY

"I'm fine Mum honestly." Louise cradled the phone between her ear and chin while tackling the washing up she didn't have time to do before getting the kids to school, she had a rare day of no appointments, so it was time to catch up on housework. Oh Joy.

"How are you anyway? How's the garden coming along?" Louise interrupted, trying to deflect the flow of the conversation.

Now this was a subject her mother could talk endlessly about and often did, with real passion. She had an ability for bringing a garden to life, choosing plants and colours complimenting each other and their surroundings; she had a real gift for it. Louise was quite envious. One day when she had time, she would love to create a real zen like space in her garden but for now it was a playground for the girls. There was a slide, trampoline, playhouse and sandpit all spaced out separately in four corners of her smallish garden, but it was big enough for them, big enough to spend a few hours playing in the summer sun keeping them occupied when the weather was nice and just an hour in the winter when it was cold because Lucy couldn't tolerate being outside too long.

Louise listened fondly to her Mum telling her of her latest spend up in the garden centre. She really couldn't resist a bargain and almost always spent over a hundred pound every time she went in. She would get so excited over the plants it was fun to be with her, watching her stepdad trying to steer her away from the more expensive items.

"So, I was thinking we could come for a visit soon, maybe in a month or so. Would that be ok?" Jane asked her daughter.

"Of course, Mum, you're welcome anytime. You know that."

Louise's Mum lived miles away in Whitby, really beautiful place but over a 6-hour drive, it was too much for Louise with both girls and having to stop at service stations, constant chattering, fights sometimes going on in the back, losing the signal for the satnav. Louise got a stomach-ache just thinking about it.

"Brilliant, we will sort out a date and let you know. But you're ok?"

"Mum I'm *fine*." Louise emphasised. Louise was nothing if not independent, probably to a fault really. She found it very difficult to ask for help and she especially didn't like worrying her mum who was so far away and couldn't do anything anyway. Well, she would come down if she needed her, but that wouldn't be fair; she had her own life to be getting on with and Louise was ok.

She really was, ok. So, some days she had to work harder than others to get out of bed, keep on top of the cooking and cleaning, the appointments, the schedule, the never ending list of chores; she had to refrain from bitch slapping certain school run mums as they breezed past her on time and looking amazing before whizzing off to their high powered job (as Louise realised she still had yesterday's socks on and couldn't remember if she had shaved both legs last night), her patience she saved just for the kids ended there and was intolerably rude to certain doctors at times, turned up at the wrong hospital for an appointment (but was at least on time), literally walked in to the kitchen and got down the pretend jar of patience she kept for emergencies whilst visualising scooping it out and patting it all over her. Cried. Sometimes cried at films, she would put a film on that was sad just so she had an excuse to cry or sometimes when she was driving unexpectedly tears would prick her eyes as her emotions rolled over after hearing something from the day she had held onto. She would drink wine on weekdays, not too much for fear of not getting up in the morning and only when the girls were asleep.

But then she laughed too, with Hayley, laughed about the shit and made fun of it, about the moments you just couldn't make up; the girls made her laugh too and made her happy and she had friends, good friends and safe places to go and to talk if she wanted to. Not that she did... but she *could*, and it felt nice being around people that felt just as unsure as you, juggling the same stuff you were, feeling a little better because you weren't on your own. She had family and a nice home.

That was everybody wasn't it? Up and down, sometimes more down, sometimes on autopilot, just functioning but not really there (those days were lonely, she hated those days).

But to sum up, she was ok, she thought. So, what was the point of moaning to her mum about it when she couldn't even pop in for a cuppa.

Louise chatted to her mum for a while, at the same time tidying up and separating the washing. She was fairly organised indoors, it felt nice. Even the postman didn't bring her any appointment letters today. Louise sat down and decided to call Hayley for a chat.

"Hi! How you doing?" Hayley seemed happy to hear from her.

"I'm good, been doing my housework, all done now so thought I'd call."

"I've done mine too and just finishing up an ironing job for a client, nice easy one today."

"Oh, shall I call back?" Louise asked her, knowing she was working.

"No, It's fine babe."

Louise could hear the squeak of the ironing board as Hayley folded it away.

"So, what's new? Heard from the guy? How was the date?" Hayley asked her.

"Hmmmm." Louise didn't sound too excited about it.

"Oh, that doesn't sound good. But that's quick even for you mate. What did he do wrong?"

"The date was nice; we had a nice time. Dinner was nice."

"Yeahhhhh?" Hayley pressed.

"I just couldn't see it going anywhere and I know you always say it doesn't have to turn in to anything but it kind of does doesn't it. Or rather I think they expect it to. I mean the date was yesterday and he has texted me 4 times since! 4 times! That's a lot."

"Babe I text you 4 times this morning! That's not a lot if you like the guy!"

"Hmmmm."

"You're just not interested, are you?"

"No. It seemed like a good idea at the time... But at the time I was a bit tipsy ..." Louise shook her head with the memory.

"Everything seems like a good idea at the time." Hayley said, making them both laugh. "Anyway, I have a confession." She told her.

"Ooh do tell."

Hayley sucked her breath in.

"I had coffee with the guy from the bar we went to yesterday."

"What?!" Louise nearly spat her coffee out. "How do I not know this already?"

"Because I didn't tell you, because I wasn't sure what I was going to do about it." Hayley laughed.

"But now you know?"

"Yes, now I know."

"And?" Louise wanted to know.

"Absolutely nothing because I have lost his number."

Hayley told Louise about coffee turning into lunch and then more coffee, how she had thought about calling him but ended up washing her jeans with the napkin on that he had written his number on for her.

"You're forgetting something." Louise told her.

"What is that?"

"If you wanted to see him again you just have to go to the gym on Monday, he told you that's when he works out right?"

"I suppose so."

"So, there you go."

"Oh, I don't know, it will be awkward and on Monday I normally have a clean, it would mean switching things around..."

"So, switch things around. When was the last time you gave anybody half a chance? Had lunch? It sounds like he is worth getting to know." Louise said it so simply, so matter of fact.

"Relationship advice? from *you*? Really?" Came the sarcastic reply.

"I'm great at advice, you know I am. My own love life may be in the shitter but doesn't mean I can't see it from other peoples view."

"Oh, I don't know."

"What have you got to lose?"

"Are you going to give Dave another chance?" Hayley countered.

"Of course!" Louise lied.

"Liar." Hayley knew her friend too well.

"You know me too well. Just because I may be terminally single doesn't mean you have to be. Rearrange your Monday."

"Maybe. Anyway, what's good looking and hangs up?" Hayley got in there quickly again before hanging up on her.

"*Damn it!*" Louise smiled at the phone.

She never beat her to it, but it always made her laugh. Louise looked at her phone, the unanswered text messages from Dave, she knew she didn't want to see him again, it was a nice date but a clear reminder that she didn't want that hassle in her life; as nice as he was, she just couldn't imagine it going any further, and she knew that was down to her but that's just the way it was for now.

Louise finally texted him back giving him the standard excuse of not being ready, but he was a lovely man and she hoped he would find someone. Then she set about planning the next play date, that always cheered her up.

CHAPTER TWENTY-ONE

They all met at a new play centre on the Saturday. Play Mania. Louise suggested getting there for 10 as soon as it opened so it wasn't as manic and could leave at lunch time, the girls were going to their dads that weekend with The Blonde. Every time she thought about it, she hated it, but what could she do? Her stomach already churning at the thought of it, would she turn up with him today? Have the grace to stay away? Louise didn't want to see her again, but it wasn't The Blonde's fault. It was no-one's fault. She sighed, the same as she told Mark, so how could she complain now?

Louise glanced at the clock; she was early again. Always bloody early, so she was left sitting waiting round for everyone else with the kids getting restless in the back of the car. She scrolled through Facebook out of boredom, stopping when seeing a new post from Jenny, it was almost a week old, but she hadn't posted since; breakfast beautifully put together by her kids and the help of their dad Chris. The tray was positioned on the bed, coffee and pancakes with a folded napkin. You could only see the tray and the satin pink pillow it sat upon. Louise smiled, that was lovely. They were such a lovely family. She was slightly envious of not having that closeness with someone, where they would look after you, let you lay in, bring you breakfast, maybe run a bath... but that kind of closeness took a certain amount of investment to get there Louise reminded herself and she wasn't prepared to do that. Jenny was lucky, she was with the man she married, the father of her kids and there was clear love there, you could see it.

Louise tapped the like button and kept on scrolling until she saw a photo from Hayley from this morning, it was of her and Flynn having a cuddle; he was smiling, not looking at her but close enough. He had his arms around her, looking very happy. Hayley was fresh faced, free of make up, but she was positively beaming, making this a beautiful photo. Louise knew how precious those moments were, making her grin with happiness for her friend.

Jenny was the next to arrive, she was only a little early. She had checked the clock a thousand times en route, worried about being late. Late would have been laughable considering the time she had been up that morning, but she had kept getting in her own way, making a hash of everything like washing up for instance; she had broken two cups and had to stop to clean it up before she could continue with the job. Chris had offered to help but she refused, he had work to do. She burnt the kids hash browns and had to make more and spilt Chris's coffee. It just wasn't going well; she had wanted to cancel; the thought of making conversation overwhelmed her but the kids were so excited to see their friends again and for that reason alone she got her act together and got them in the car.

Hayley pulled up just after, she was clearly frazzled and walked immediately to the back of her car lighting a cigarette so the boys couldn't see.

"One-minute girls." Louise got out to say hello and see what was bothering her friend.

"Hey, you alright mate?" Louise approached Hayley looking concerned. Hayley shook her head, tears escaping while she took a long drag on her cigarette.

"What a fucking morning!" She began "I'll be alright in a minute, just needed this you know."

Hayley took two more drags then stubbed it out, blowing the smoke out in a long breath.

"Flynn did a poo just before we left, it was everywhere. Had to do a complete change and wash which he hates. He wanted a bath, and we didn't have time and I'm trying to stay upbeat the whole time then he kicks me in the face. Full on in the face." She took a deep breath "Everything was fine until then, we were having a lovely morning, it just took a turn."

"I know I saw the photo; it was beautiful mate." Louise put her hand on Hayley's arm.

"Yeah, it was." Hayley smiled. "I'm ok." She sighed deeply, "Just being a drama queen."

"You're allowed to moan about being kicked in the face. That must have been stressful, just about to go out the. door and having to strip him off completely." Louise empathised.

"You know what he's like when he knows he's going soft play, he loves it and so excited he was. He thought we weren't going when I had to change him, so totally kicked off. I couldn't get his clothes off; he was fighting me even when I kept saying nappy change first soft play after. He couldn't hear me cos he was yelling so loud! All I could smell was shit, I can still smell it now! Can you smell it?"

"No mate, not at all. Let's go and let off some steam eh."

"Yeah, thanks mate. I'll be ok now."

Jenny sat and watched the exchange between the two friends and her heart went out to Hayley. She had no idea what had upset her like that, but she knew from experience that whatever it was she wouldn't want a stranger (or someone she hardly knew) approaching while she was trying to get herself together, so Jenny stayed in the car for a few more minutes then joined them inside.

The play centre was big, bigger than the one they were used to and for a minute Louise was unsure about it.

"It'll be fine babe." Hayley reassured her. "One of us goes with Sam and Amy and the other one stays with Lucy and Flynn."

Louise nodded "Ok. I'll stay with Lucy and Flynn."

They had the spinny thing that Flynn liked and a slide that Lucy could manage plus a sensory area joining on to the small soft play part they would both like and a ball pit area too. This was nice, manageable.

Sam and Amy were already off, kicking their shoes off as they ran, spotting the big slide. Hayley ran after them.

"Wait for me." She called laughing.

"Hi Louise." Jenny's voice broke into her thoughts.

"Hi!" Louise stood up; she had shut herself in the small play area letting them two crawl around for a moment.

"Good to see you, how are you doing?" Louise leant over the barrier to kiss Jenny's cheek.

"Oh, I'm ok." Jenny replied smiling. She looked relaxed in leggings and a long blue top that came above her knees, a pastel pink scarf hanging loosely round her neck. "Would you like a coffee?" She asked.

"Oh no thanks, I can't take it in here because of the little ones." Louise explained. They were the only ones here at the moment but that wouldn't last too long.

"I don't mind swapping over while you have a coffee, mine have run off, I feel a bit redundant." Jenny said looking towards the play area for the older children; Paul and Mia had sprinted towards shrieking in excitement when they had seen the big slide and Hayley, Sam and Amy all in a row about to go down. Hayley was grinning, Louise really thought she loved the slides more than the kids sometimes!

"That would be great, thanks." Louise began spinning Flynn on the padded pole as he gripped it, his head upwards, mouth open in a silent laugh. Lucy was determinedly climbing the little steps towards the slide. This was a safe area for them, no bigger kids pushing them out of the way (Unintentionally of course, but in excitement) It was really meant for babies and toddlers but It's where they were all comfortable and was far more suited to their needs; they were small for their age too, so nobody really batted an eyelid. Sometimes you got a few people that would stare, but you always got that, and God help them if Hayley noticed it!

Jenny came back with two coffees on a tray, some sugar and milk; setting it down on a red round table next to the enclosed toddler area.

"I bought some sugar; I wasn't sure if you had it or not." Jenny said.

"Oh yes, strong and sweet that's how I like my coffee." Louise said, inhaling the smell of caffeine, it smelled good.

"I like mine a little cooler, why don't you come and have yours and I'll watch them two." Jenny offered.

"Are you sure?"

"Absolutely." Jenny was already taking off her boots.

"Thank you." Louise said appreciatively, stopping spinning Flynn who immediately moaned in protest.

"It's ok, I'll spin you Flynn." Jenny sat down next to him and started spinning. Louise watched her, she seemed happier with a job to do and was smiling at Flynn, Lucy was laughing as she pushed herself off the slide again, she could hear Hayley shrieking along with the kids, thoroughly enjoying herself and now

Louise felt redundant, but she managed to take some photos of Lucy and Flynn, some nice ones, then after finishing her coffee she went back into the toddler area to take over from Jenny.

"Go and have your coffee Jenny," Louise knelt down to take over "Before it gets too cold."

Jenny did so, then took a walk checking on Paul and Mia as the play centre began to fill up. There was a birthday party group arriving; about 30 kids with their parents; the kids piled in trying to contain their obvious excitement and stay in a line as their party host counted heads. Birthday bags and balloons attached to the child dressed in their best outfit as they headed to the party room headed by the party host, closely followed by the stressed-out mum carrying the cake and the big number 6 helium balloon, wearing a thin smile and wincing at the kids screams behind her, trying and failing to hear what the party host was saying before they kicked away their shoes running off to play. Louise looked up to see where Sam and Amy were, but knew they would be ok with Hayley.

Jenny came walking back soon after too, Paul and Mia were happily navigating the big play frame by themselves in no need of Mum, she really did feel redundant. Sitting at the table by herself felt rude and following the kids round when they were doing ok without her seemed overprotective, so she came into the toddler area again and sat with Louise.

"They're doing ok, Paul and Mia, aren't they?" Louise observed.

"Yeah, they've always been climbers, loved play equipment. It's kind of one thing I don't have to worry about really." Jenny said still watching that area.

"Well, that's nice isn't it. We have enough to worry about as it is." Louise laughed "One less thing is always welcome!"

"True," Jenny smiled "Here, I can spin for a while if you want, your arms must be getting tired."

"They are, I don't know how Hayley does it for so long." Louise stopped, glad of the offer.

"Practice I suppose. She works out too doesn't she." Jenny remarked.

"Yeah, I wish I enjoyed exercise the way she did." Louise patted her stomach.

"What?! Don't be daft, there's nothing of you." Jenny exclaimed.

"thanks, but I know I've put on weight."

"Nonsense, you look great Louise." Jenny told her.

"Thank you," Louise said gratefully "I still feel like a bag of worms most days." She joked "You always look so good, like you really have it all together."

Jenny laughed a short laugh in surprise, she didn't know how to respond. That was certainly what she wanted everyone to think, but it wasn't how she felt. Not at all.

They were interrupted by a puffing and red Hayley.

"Well, you look nice and comfy." She joked, coming into the toddler area to join them. "Hi Jenny."

"Hi Hayley." Jenny was slowly getting used to Hayley's jokes.

"I'll go over and see to them." Louise started getting up.

"They're on the big balls, you know the one where you push them along on the rope, it's as you go through on the left." Hayley told her pointing to the left of the play frame.

"Ok got it." Louise walked off leaving Hayley and Jenny together.

"Paul and Mia are lovely babe; they were so helpful in there! Amy got stuck in a tunnel. Couldn't get my fat ass in. I tried! So, they went in either side to help." Hayley began spinning Flynn again and again "Has he been on this the whole time? He loves it so much!" Hayley laughed.

"Yes, he has." Jenny told her, watching Lucy now climbing into the ball pit, holding up the balls looking at each colour. Jenny sat with her watching her and helping her move about when she wanted to go to the other side.

"They love playing with the kids, they find it hard to make friends," Jenny confided, "They were so excited about today."

"Ahh that's nice, Sam was too. He loves Amy and they all got on so well together at the woods didn't they so was looking forward to seeing Paul and Mia again. It's good for them to have friends, they need it. Just like us really." Hayley carried on spinning, Flynn was finally bored and made his way to the slide. Lucy saw him, she tried to climb out of the ball pit to join but needed a little help, so Jenny picked her up and got her out. She nodded at Hayley's comment but said nothing.

"Talking of which," Hayley added, seeing an opportunity. "We're having drinks at mine tonight when kids are asleep, just some nibbles and a few glasses of wine. Why don't you come? It will just be me and Louise." She explained seeing the panicked look on Jenny's face.

"Oh-I-I don't know. I'm not sure what plans Chris may have made." Jenny responded, feeling hot all of a sudden. Jenny never socialised without the kids. Never. In the early days Chris had tried to take her out on special occasions; birthdays and anniversary's and after jumping through the many hoops she put in the way and smoothing out any problems that Jenny would foresee, she would agree to a dinner but it was clear she was there only in body; constantly checking her phone, calling Chris's mum twice to see if everything was ok, eating quickly to be able to leave early and not joining in with any conversation Chris made attempts at, he finally gave up and they simply celebrated at home instead or took the children with them.

"Oh, does he go out some weekends Hun?" Hayley asked casually, but she was probing.

"Oh, not really, but he may have planned dinner or something." Jenny's excuses were tame, and she knew it. Hayley didn't want to push her, but she was perceptive and could see Jenny needed to unwind and could do with some friends and even a life outside of the kids.

"Ok no worries. But if you change your mind, offer is there!" She smiled widely showing Jenny she meant it "It's just nice to have a glass of wine and adult conversation sometimes."

Jenny nodded, part of her longed for the unity of friendship again, seeing how close Louise and Hayley were, was lovely. A real bond. She had that once, with Chris. It felt like a betrayal somehow, she couldn't even let him close to her anymore, slowly over the years all that they had shared had worn down to just what they had in common now and that was the house, mealtimes and the kids and even that Jenny took control of. She couldn't even begin to imagine not being in control, of not being there when they went to bed-how they went to bed, the routine leading up to the bedtime, the meals they ate, bath times, making sure they had their vitamins, their physio. No, she had not been in control when they were born, she had let them down then and she never would again, never. She would always be there. It was her job.

"What's the matter?!" Hayley exclaimed seeing Louise rushing toward her with all four kids in tow.

"Erm-We're leaving!" She flustered, looking quite concerned.

Jenny turned to see what was wrong and Louise pointed to a poor child crying to his mother looking extremely uncomfortable and the horrified shrieks that followed as his mother realised what he was covered in, even around his poor neck.

"Someone has had an accident down the slide." Louise said slowly "And by accident, I mean the kind of diarrhoea that only explodes when someone is really ill, then other kids went down after him. It's all in the ball pit at the bottom. It's everywhere."

"Oh My God." Jenny got up, grabbing her bottle of sanitiser immediately covering all the children's hands in it "Here you too Louise."

"Thankyou." She said gratefully, if only she had thought to bring hers., from now on it will be on the list.

Shoes were put on double fast. Thankfully all kids had had a lovely time so far and didn't mind leaving especially as it was now approaching lunchtime.

"I think I'm going to sling mine in the bath when we get home just to be on the safe side." Hayley said.

"Me too." Louise and Jenny both agreed.

"Right text you later girls." Hayley called as they all hurried off to their own cars. "Shit just follows me everywhere." She said to herself and laughed at the irony of it.

CHAPTER TWENTY-TWO

"What was all down the slide?!" Chris asked incredulously, hardly believing his ears.

Normally Jenny wouldn't mention anything about their day, but the kids couldn't stop thinking about it, signing 'poo' and giggling together at the dinner table inviting questions from Chris who literally couldn't believe what he heard.

"Oh, that's awful!" He screwed his face up. "I mean poor kid as well though, that's got to be really embarrassing and you said a boy went down the slide right after him?"

Jenny nodded not wanting to explain any further, the image of that poor boy with someone else's poo smeared down his neck and body made her shudder.

"Poo." Paul said, making Mia giggle again.

"Let's talk about something else, shall we?" Jenny suggested. She had driven home, scooping them in the bath as fast as was humanly possible, making sure there was nothing in the car as well.

"Did they close the play centre?" Chris enquired, spooning some potatoes onto his plate. It wasn't the best subject, but it made a nice change to be at least talking at the dinner table for once.

"Do you know, I don't know." Jenny thought for a moment "We just all got out as soon as we could. Thank God Louise saw it happen or they could have all gone down afterwards as well." Chris could see Jenny thinking "They must have closed up afterwards, surely you would have to. Well, they *should* have, that is a health and hygiene issue, the place needs a deep clean."

Chris smiled; it had been a long time since he had seen Jenny become animated about anything that wasn't the kids.

"You're right" He said encouraging her "What was the place like anyway? Any good?"

"I prefer the other one, Monkey Madness. It's smaller but more manageable and..."

"Cleaner?" Chris offered, smiling.

Jenny smiled too "Yes. Definitely cleaner. Depends on the clientele though."

Chris laughed. He felt very sorry for the poor child who had been unwell today and even more so for the unsuspecting child who had slid straight into it and for both their parents having to deal with the aftermath but in a strange way he was glad as well; this had been the first time in a very long time they had had a decent conversation about anything, and he welcomed it. Eating in silence was awkward and lonely, only sharing snippets of their day out of politeness and information about Paul and Mia the other needed to know. Well, that was mainly Jenny telling Chris something important about the kids. She didn't mean to exclude him as such but had successfully organised everything so that she could deal with all aspects of their life alone, never asking for help. She would be the best mother she could be, and no one would say any different. This inbuilt fear stemmed from their birth and the guilt that had been born along with the twins that only seemed to grow with them as she watched them struggle with day-to-day activities that others picked up so easily, the friendships they had trouble forming and the communication they found so difficult where others naturally learned. This guilt that throbbed and ebbed inside of her, blamed her for all these things; for not keeping them safe inside her protective womb long enough so they would have been born with a better chance. She may have failed them and Chris too at the job she should have done so well but she wouldn't fail at being their mother, providing for them the way they needed. That was her only goal in life now.

"It's nice the way you've all made friends with each other. They sound like nice kids." Chris said to Jenny, wanting to continue the conversation.

"When will you be seeing them again?" He wanted to know.

"Oh, I'm not sure. It will be nice to get the kids together again, they have so much fun together. I took some photos. Do you want to see?" Jenny slid her phone across the table to him and Chris eagerly looked through the photos, wanting to be more a part of their days.

"They look great. So happy."

Jenny nodded, looking at Paul and Mia. It had been a good day, they had been happy playing with their friends, a real sense of belonging... until it had been cut short, but there would be another time Jenny found herself hoping.

"The mums look nice too. What are their names again?"

"Hayley and Louise. They are nice." Jenny agreed "Funny too, always bickering but in a good-natured way."

Chris noticed a softening of his wife then; she looked a little wistful like she was missing something.

"You could always invite them here one evening if you like," He ventured "It's nice to have friends' round, would be nice for you."

Chris missed what they used to share, that special tie that only they had. It had been him and her against the world, he could live his life happy in her laughter, only needing her and the way she used to kiss him, wear his shirts first thing in the morning to get his coffee, her hair a mess, no make-up and not caring. He had thought she had never been more beautiful when she was heavily pregnant with the twins, in one of his old work shirts, half buttoned up with a vest underneath and a pair of shorts, leaning against the fridge at 4 in the morning spooning ice cream right out of the tub. That had been 4 days before Paul and Mia were born and one of his most precious memories of her. He hadn't seen a glimpse of that person since; that happy, carefree, openly loving woman. He wanted so much to share special moments with her again but maybe what she needed right now was friends and maybe that wasn't him, as much as that hurt him to admit.

"Oh," Jenny looked a little flustered "Oh that's ok. They did invite me over there tonight because Louise has the night off and Hayley is doing some nibbles, but I said no."

"No? How come?" Chris knew how come, that she wasn't open to things like that but was pushing it and he knew it.

"I didn't think I should just make those kinds of plans without checking with you first." That was lame and they both knew it. Jenny made all the plans for them both, she organised their lives to perfection. Chris smiled and nodded.

"You don't have to check with me, and I hope you didn't tell them that, they will think I'm a cave man!" He scoffed.

"No. No I didn't" She looked a little embarrassed now. "And of course you're not."

Jenny stood up to clear the plates away, busying herself but Chris saw his opportunity, following her into the kitchen while the kids were still eating.

"So why don't you go?" He asked quietly. Gently reaching out to touch her arm, hoping she wouldn't pull away. This would be good for her he thought, to make some friends, maybe open up to somebody. Lord knew she wouldn't open up to him as much as he wished she would, for her to even laugh with someone else and have fun would be good for her even though he wished it was him who could help her do that, he loved her so damn much he just wanted her to be happy.

"Well, I need to put the kids to bed and then I'll probably be too tired." She insisted pulling away and stacking the dishwasher.

"Jenny." Chris said so softly that she turned to look at him. "Please go. I want to put the kids to bed and read to them, it would be nice for me to do that for a change, and I think it would be good for you too. Besides it's not a bad idea to keep friendly with them because the kids are all getting on so well, we want to make sure they keep their friendships too."

It was a bit manipulative, and he knew it, hating himself for it, but if anything would work that would. He watched Jenny blink back tears as she nodded.

"Ok." She agreed.

Chris grinned. "Great! You go and have fun, darling you deserve it." He leant forward kissing her cheek as delicately as though he were handling a butterfly's wing, terrified to damage it. She may seem tough and intimidating to some, but he knew just how fragile she was.

Louise squealed happily after Jenny entered holding a bottle of Sauvignon blanc dressed in black trousers and a beige rollneck jumper, her blonde hair cascading across her shoulders as though she had just stepped out of a hairdressers.

"Oh, I'm so glad you came!" Louise jumped up to welcome her, giving her a kiss on the cheek. Jenny was becoming a little more used to Hayley and Louise's affection and tried not to flinch.

"I've got one open babe; shall I pour you a glass of that or do you want the one you brought?" Hayley asked.

"The open one is fine." Jenny answered, sitting down stiffly on the comfy sofa, looking around.

"The place is lovely Hayley; did you decorate yourself?" She asked.

Hayley was good at putting colours together, she had a natural flair for it.

"Sure did." Hayley came back carrying Jenny's glass of wine. There were nibbles on a small table in between the chairs as promised and candles lit on the windowsills, a lovely aroma of chocolate and cinnamon surrounded them.

"It smells lovely in here." Jenny commented.

"Oh, does it? Good." Hayley looked relieved. "Those are my new Yankee candles I just love them; they really fill the room with their scent."

Jenny accepted the glass of wine, sipping it slowly, enjoying its taste. She could certainly do with it.

"How did the kids get off today babe? You never got round to telling me." Hayley asked Louise.

Louise looked agitated being reminded by it.

"Yeah ok. We didn't argue this time and *she* didn't come which was good."

Jenny looked questioningly at Louise, sipping more of her wine trying to relax a bit.

"The girls dad." Louise began to explain.

"Oh, you don't have to explain." Jenny began.

"No, it's ok I don't mind." Louise said honestly. "We broke up a long time ago just after Amy was born and it's been difficult between us ever since. He is bloody minded, doesn't listen to half the things I say, see's them once a fortnight which is ok with me, we arranged it that way." Louise looked down into her wine glass before continuing, "But recently he has been having the girls overnight because he's moved into a bigger place and two weeks ago when he dropped them off there was a woman in the car with them."

Jenny's mouth dropped open "Oh." She said, understanding Louise's angst immediately.

"Yeah exactly. No warning, no notice, no conversation previous to picking the kids up... which he could have done! Even a text for god's sake and when I called him on it, he tells me it's not a fling It's a serious relationship and they are living together but didn't think he had to let me know. So now the girls are spending time with her all weekend while they are with him."

"Oh, I'm sorry Louise." Jenny sympathised.

"Yeah, thanks. I know I have no right to say anything, we have been broken up over 5 years, but it just sucks knowing they're playing happy families together."

"I can imagine." Jenny nodded, draining her glass, beginning to relax a little now and letting Hayley pour her another.

"Are you sure you don't have any feelings for him still babe? You seem so upset by it." Hayley asked.

"No, I really don't! It's just, I don't know, reminds me of how I haven't moved on and how easy it was for him to do I guess."

"Do you *want* to move on? 'Cos you could if you wanted to. What about that guy?" Hayley sat down on the other end of the sofa picking up some peanuts.

Jenny was interested- there was a guy?

Louise shook her head "No. I made some excuse; I won't be seeing him again. We had dinner; it was nice but- no."

Jenny was flabber ghasted. Louise was dating! After everything she had to do and she went on dates too, she could hardly believe it. How did she manage to juggle it?

"You're a nightmare." Hayley shook her head at Louise.

"You're not much better!" She accused light heartedly "At least I actually go on the dates."

Jenny feeling much more relaxed and amused now felt she could join in on the conversation.

"Ok, so you need to fill me in, who is this guy?"

Louise and Hayley filled Jenny in on their last night out, the guys they met and the phone numbers that were exchanged between Louise and Dave, leading to Louise texting him when she was still tipsy and then going on the date. Louise made Jenny laugh with her impression of Hayley dancing like Kylie Minogue after a few drinks.

"Oh, you should come with us next time!" Hayley told her.

"Oh, it's been years since I've been out like that." Jenny shook her head.

"Which is exactly why you need to come," Louise added. "Even if it is just to witness the marvel that is Kylie."

Jenny laughed "Does sound fun" She admitted, allowing Hayley to fill her glass up again along with the others. "Are the boys asleep?" She asked.

"My folks offered to pick them up for me so they could stay overnight. They're good like that." She smiled. "Do your parents babysit much Jenny?"

"Umm no. Not really, we just tend to have evenings in, you know what it's like when your busy with the kids."

"Oh yeah," Louise agreed. "It's finding the energy too, but I think it's still important to have that bit of time to yourself. You know, remind yourself who you are. Amy asked me the other day what my favourite song was, and do you know what I couldn't answer her! Just couldn't think of a song that I loved that wasn't a song I listen to with the girls."

"Oh, mate I get that. Whenever I put on a tv programme, they're in here moaning so I turn it over and when they're in bed I don't even want the telly on!" Hayley shook her head "They are my whole world you know, but it's nice sometimes to just have adult conversation." She looked a little sheepish then before adding "I had a little adult conversation on Monday."

Jenny looked intrigued.

"Meaning??"

"Well, I was having a workout at the gym, don't usually go on Mondays do I, but things changed so thought I may as well, I found myself down there and who do I see looking my way?"

"Who?" Jenny asked expectantly.

"Simon. The guy from the bar" Hayley told her.

"Oh really? What happened?" Jenny wanted to know; Louise sat quietly after already hearing about it in the week. It still surprised her now. He must have made a real impression on her friend.

"Well, I almost blew him off, I mean he approached me mid work out, so I was not looking my best-I know it's hard to imagine." Hayley flicked her hair and winked, making Jenny and Louise laugh. "But he seemed so nice and genuine, so I agreed to coffee. Then coffee turned in to lunch and I ended up spending all afternoon with him and almost being late for the school run. We just hit it off."

"Wow, that's great Hayley." Jenny was genuinely pleased for her.

"It's brilliant." Louise added "I mean I'm over the moon, but I am surprised. He must have made a good impression on you; you never do that".

"I know. To be honest I almost told him to fuck off, but something stopped me, and we ended up having a lovely time together."

"So, have you called him?" Jenny wanted to know.

"No." Hayley sighed. "I don't have time for this in my life, the odd night out is not the same as planning regular dates and it's the disappointment when it goes wrong."

"But it doesn't have to go wrong." Louise argued. "Sometimes it goes right. I mean look at Jenny; she's the perfect example of happily married. It does work sometimes mate."

Jenny felt her chest tighten. Her marriage was far from perfect, but again that's what she wanted people to see and so that's what they saw.

"Are *you* the serial dumper seriously giving *me* relationship advice?" Hayley raised an eyebrow.

"I can give advice, I'm *good* at giving advice." Louise grinned "Just not taking it." She sipped her wine, "But you're a little like that," She joked "Remember what you said? Not everything has to turn in to a serious relationship does it?"

Hayley pulled a face "I couldn't call him even If I wanted to." She admitted. "I had his number on a napkin in my pocket and I washed them, it's disintegrated into tiny bits."

"Oh no." Jenny sympathised "Can't you just go down to the gym on a Monday again and explain." She suggested logically.

"See? Both of us can't be wrong." Louise sat back smugly.

"I don't know, maybe." Hayley considered it "I'll think about it. Anyway, let's get some tunes on and stop talking about my love life or lack of!"

Hayley fiddled with her phone, connecting it to the speakers and 'We Are Family' by Sister Sledge came on.

"Wow this is a blast from the past!" Louise grinned singing along.

"I used to love this song!" Jenny was caught in a moment of nostalgia when she was younger dancing to this song with another group of friends before she had met Chris, brought back to the present by Hayley wiggling her bum and singing into a hairbrush, she giggled, beginning to sing along as well. This was a very different set of friends but ones she was finding an affinity with, she was glad she came, and Jenny laughed, sang old tunes with them and drank wine until it was midnight and her cab turned up.

"Goodnight Cinderella." Hayley hugged Jenny goodbye; Louise was already half asleep on the sofa. She hated going home to an empty house she had told them earlier. Hayley already knew this and had leant her the sofa many times before. True friendship this was, Jenny thought and hugged her back.

"Goodnight Kylie." Jenny waved as she climbed into her cab.

CHAPTER TWENTY-THREE

Housework done, a long soak in the bath and half a pack of biscuits later, Louise was bored. She didn't always like daytime TV, and she was on top of everything else- for a change! The girls weren't due back for another two hours now and when they did come back it was too late for anything except dinner. She had missed them and wished it was 4 pm already. Her stomach turned over already thinking about Mark's car pulling up and that woman in the front. Mark hadn't even introduced her, wasn't that rude, shouldn't she at least have been introduced?! She wondered what they were doing and how much fun they had had together all weekend, they got to do all the fun stuff and not the boring day to day *parent* stuff that kept them well. Louise sighed, she must stop obsessing over this; her hands twitched restlessly, picking up her phone for a moment thinking of texting Dave. NO! She scolded herself, just because you're bored! You can't start things up again, you would only have to dump him all over again! And that hadn't been easy, Louise exhaled remembering the umpteen texts he had sent asking what he had done wrong- some really didn't go easy.

Hayley was right, she *was* a serial dumper, a complete commitment-phobe, not able to see past the first two or even three dates before something freaked her out or she made an excuse. Nope things were fine just as they were and if Mark had moved on then she should be happy for him and she would try, she really would. It would be healthy for them to try and be pleasant with each other when the girls were dropped off and picked up.

An hour and a half left, maybe she could make a start on dinner ready for when they got home but Louise's itchy feet wouldn't let her focus on anything in the fridge, staring at the items on the shelves waiting for something to jump out and inspire her. Wouldn't it be nice to just go out? Well, why couldn't they? That would be nice to just go out for dinner, she usually only took them out to dinner on special occasions but why not, it would be a nice treat for them and her too. Impulsively, Louise grabbed the phone calling TGI Fridays and booking a table for 4:30. She couldn't wait for them to come home now, she would be waiting outside ready for them and could go straight away. Happy with her plan, Louise went upstairs to change into something more suited to dinner out. Jeans (Clean, ironed jeans) and her favourite pale blue fitted tunic with boots, it suited Louise and she felt comfortable in it.

She was waiting for them at 4 pm in the car and for once Mark was on time, thankfully. She went over to meet them, noting that he hadn't brought his friend along this time.

"Hi girls." She sang opening the door, eager for a cuddle "Did you have a nice time?"

Amy clambered out wrapping her arms around Louise, tears in her eyes. Lucy was still struggling with her belt and Mark tried to help her.

"Honey, what's wrong?" Louise tried to look at Amy, but she kept hiding her face in Louise's leg.

"Why is Amy upset?" Louise asked Mark.

"Oh, I dunno, she's tired that's all." He shrugged and helped Lucy out of the car.

"Did she have a late night then?" Louise asked.

"Nah not really, about 10."

"10! That's very late for her Mark! She goes to bed at 7 the latest normally."

"Well, I don't get to see them often do I. So, I want to make the most of it."

"So, you stop being a responsible parent because you selfishly want her to stay up late. And I'm guessing she was up early too."

"About 6." Mark held his hands up. "She was excited! What am I supposed to apologise for that as well am I?! Jeez."

Mark put the girl's bags on the floor while Louise comforted Amy, Lucy hugged Louise then he got in the car and started the engine.

Louise peeled Amy off her for a second, putting her head through his open passenger door window "You utter prick," She seethed. "I've got both of them clinging to me and you can't even walk the bags down to the door like a decent human being."

Mark looked down a little shamefaced and went to open his door.

"No, go ahead and fuckoff. I've got this. As always." She told him quietly so the girls wouldn't hear.

Louise picked Lucy up knowing she was tired too and wouldn't be able to walk down to the front door, held Amy to her and slowly took them to her car ignoring the bags, she would get them in a minute.

"Where are we going Mummy?" Amy asked confused.

"Out for dinner. Would you like burger and chips for dinner tonight?" She asked smiling trying to inject a little enthusiasm.

"Yes!" Lucy loved burgers and was grinning from ear to ear now at the mention of it.

Amy nodded but wasn't as enthusiastic as Lucy, in fact she looked a little pale.

"Are you feeling ok Amy? Do you want to go out for dinner?"

Amy nodded "I'm ok, yes please Mummy." Her tiny voice melted Louise and she kissed her forehead, clicking them both in safely, she retrieved the bags from the floor, putting them in the boot. She was still fuming from Mark and the way he had handed the children over; there was no information, nothing. Had they had a good time, eaten well, had a bath last night, anything at all. She tried to push it all to the back of her mind and enjoy the time with the girls now, chattering away to them constantly as she drove to the restaurant. Amy was a little subdued, but she would be wouldn't she, after a late night and early morning, it wasn't surprising at all. She would hopefully perk up a little when she got there. They both loved TGI Fridays.

Dinner was lovely, their waitress made a special effort with the girls, bringing them colouring in pens and pads, balloons and telling them how lovely they looked, and they did look lovely; Amy's curls escaped her hair band and danced round her face, her usually bright and cheerful face but as much as she tried, she wasn't herself. She was wearing the long-sleeved yellow dress Louise had packed, with thick white tights and black ankle boots, Lucy was wearing her blue and white pinstriped strappy dress with a white top underneath and thick white tights, her hair was plaited today, and Louise knew Mark couldn't do that; she tried not to imagine The Blonde's fingers in her daughter's hair.

Lucy as usual demolished her burger and chips, dipping every mouthful in to her tomato ketchup first. Lucy had tomato ketchup with everything, she loved it. Amy was quiet still and was still struggling with her dinner when Louise and Lucy had finished.

"You ok babe?" Louise rested the back of her hand on Amy's forehead testing her temperature – she didn't feel hot; then Amy began to gag, and Louise knew instinctively she was going to be sick. They had no time to get to the bathroom so she cupped her hands together, reaching forward as quick as she could catching the vomit that inevitably came up. Louise's hands were full of warm lumpy sick, she was so glad she had caught it and it wasn't all over the table but what was she supposed to do with it now?!

She knew people were watching but tried to ignore them, scanning the table for anything she could use. The empty glass was the only thing, carefully Louise poured the sick into the empty glass, catching the horrified waitress's eye as she hurried past.

"Bill please!" She called.

A packet of baby wipes later, the bill paid, and a nice tip left for the poor waitress who had to deal with their table, Louise was ready to leave.

"Here you go." The waitress bought over a small chocolate for both the girls "For when you're feeling better." She added to Amy.

"Thank you," Louise said gratefully. "Very sorry." She added, gesturing to the table as she picked up a very pale looking Amy and hoped Lucy would be able to walk to the car, she had left the buggy in it thinking she wouldn't need it; usually it was Lucy she picked up and Amy walked.

Lucy loved chocolate and immediately began unwrapping it, popping it into her mouth delightfully, then spitting it out almost as soon as she put it in with a loud "YUCK!" Dark chocolate. Oops, they both hated dark chocolate.

Definitely time to go. Louise walked out of the restaurant not looking back, or meeting anybody's eyes as they stared, vowing to not go there again for quite some time.

CHAPTER TWENTY-FOUR

The following weekend brought the beginning of December and with it a real cold snap. The weather had been minus 2 since Thursday, the forecast predicted snow this weekend. As usual, the first weekend in December meant the Christmas decorations were to be put up so all of Saturday, Jenny, Chris, Paul and Mia decorated their beautiful 7 foot tree, placed to the left of the fireplace with red and gold baubles, continuing the red and gold theme with a garland around the fireplace, a red and gold wreath on their front door, Christmas candles adorned the table and a 4 foot Santa and his reindeer in lights in the front garden.

The day brought fresh excitement for Paul and Mia, Jenny put on Christmas music while they decorated and made them hot chocolate when they were finished. Making sure the tree was just right and the garland was exactly hanging the same on each end, she called them all over for the yearly Christmas photo. Setting the timer, Jenny hurried back in place in front of the fireplace with Chris next to her and the kids in front. Jenny wearing a red skirt, white blouse, her hair swept across one shoulder, Chris in his usual jeans and a white shirt, Paul in jeans too and a red t-shirt, Mia wearing a red dress. Jenny had wanted Chris in a red shirt too, but he had insisted he didn't have one to hand. She knew he did, she had ironed it herself and it irked her, but she didn't push it. The red theme would have flowed far better if he had just worn it.

They posed for the picture, smiling, all looking picture perfect. After Jenny had checked it and was happy, they could disperse. Paul and Mia happy to go and play while Jenny saw to the dinner.

"Snow! Snow!" Mia jumped up and down at the sight of the first snowflakes falling, they were drifting down slowly at first, then with more determined force until it was heavily snowing.

"Wow!" Paul said in awe. The last time it had snowed had been two years ago, and that was only a light flurry not really settling. This was really coming down now. Mia whooped in excitement, ran to the cupboard to find her wellies and falling over in the process.

"Let me help." Chris chuckled.

They all stood in the garden, looking up at the falling snow; letting it hit their skin. Paul tried to catch them on his tongue and laughed when he felt it there, Mia copied, then held her hands out catching them on her gloves examining them.

"Snow." She breathed.

Jenny signed snow for them to copy, Chris watched on with his heart full of love for his family. This couldn't have been a more perfect time to happen, he took his phone out and snapped a photo of the twins looking upwards in awe and Jenny looking on with warmth.

Dinner had been lovely, Jenny had made lasagne with salad and garlic bread, they all loved it and ate every bit, Paul and Mia tired from playing in the garden but still excited because the snow hadn't stopped falling and was really settling now; a thin sheet of white beginning to cover the ground.

As they cleared away the plates, Chris went to help in the kitchen while Paul and Mia ate some yogurt for afters.

"I think there will be a lot more snow tonight, that would be great wouldn't it, to make a snowman in the morning." Chris said to Jenny.

"Oh, I hope so." Jenny replied, genuinely excited too. Snow brought out the kid in everyone and they were all in good spirits that evening.

"You know I was thinking tonight, maybe we could both read to the kids and put them to bed together." He suggested boldly. Chris had felt like an outsider looking in with the children for so long now, Jenny taking care of everything without batting an eye, doing jobs without asking for help, getting the kids needs met before he had a chance to help, and he had been missing out. He wanted to do these things, wanted to be closer to them all, join the bubble she seemed to create and after her night out last week it had been just them three; he had got them bathed, ready for bed and read to them. Every moment of it he had cherished and made him realise he had been missing out; the kids too, they had giggled and snuggled in for their stories. Chris wanted to tuck them in every night but didn't want to take that away from Jenny either.

He saw her stiffen a little, then smile her polite smile that never reached her eyes and nodded.

"That would be lovely." She allowed her smile to deepen to show she meant it and carried on clearing up.

"Great," Chris grinned, feeling happier than he had in a long time, leaving the room to tell the kids. "Thanks".

Jenny looked up to see Chris looking at her from the doorway of their bright, big kitchen. His eyes tinged with tears, his kind face showing the unwavering love he felt for her and her heart skipped. Oh, she loved him so! Why wouldn't these legs walk over there for her head to rest upon his chest, to smell him so close to her and feel his arms around her again, his soft hands running his fingers through her hair. She longed for his touch again, but rooted to the spot, Jenny stood there woodenly watching him turn and leave.

The kids *were* excited. Chris had been right to suggest it. He joined them not just for bedtime but for the bath too. They splashed each other in joy, blowing the bubbles over each other, joining in some of the words Jenny sang, being wrapped in the big soft towel afterwards by Chris and dried off, both of them helping with their pyjamas.

They still shared a room and had an adjoining room as a playroom. The plan was in the next year or so they would change the playroom and give them both their own bedrooms.

Putting the soft light on and looking through the books to choose one, Paul and Mia had already picked one up, the same one as Chris had read them the week before she noticed. Paul handed it to Chris, climbed into bed and waited. His big expectant brown eyes shining with love for his Father. Mia too had her eyes on Chris, waiting patiently for him to start reading and when he did Jenny knew why. He was a natural; Chris read slowly and deliberately, pausing in the right places, acting out the story and changing his voice for the characters making the kids giggle. Jenny looked on feeling redundant but happy for them to be having this special moment. She didn't read with that passion and commitment, she just read; yet Chris was in his element and they didn't miss her at the bed side at all. She had been selfish wanting all this to herself for so long and excluding him, she knew it and she had probably hurt Chris in the process too without meaning to; she just wanted to keep them so close but look at them now! They were cuddled together, Paul and Mia hanging onto each and every word Chris said, knowing the story already but it was like they were hearing it for the first time.

They don't need you. Jenny tried to shake it off, but the voiceless words kept coming.

They don't need you. Jenny focused on her family, trying to ignore it,

They don't need you. It wouldn't stop.

They don't need you.

Jenny left the room, fighting the gremlin who had crawled into her head, she undressed and got into bed, pulling the covers over her; not wanting Chris to see the pain in her face nor question her leaving. Her eyes squeezed shut, she listened to him finishing his story and telling the twins he loved them, closing their door gently before padding along the hallway wondering where she was.

"Jenny?" He called quietly seeing her shape in the bed and feeling confused. Why had she not stayed? or even kissed the kid's goodnight? She had never not kissed them goodnight, perhaps she had had one of her sudden headaches or wanted to give them some space seeing as Chris didn't usually get to put them to bed... but even so Chris was perplexed.

"Jenny?" He tried again, reaching out to touch the covers.

"I have a headache." Her strained voice came back at him.

"Shall I get you some tablets?" He offered.

"No. No thank you."

"Ok, I'll leave you be then." Chris left the room, his earlier good mood now gone, he didn't think she had a headache, he knew it was to do with sharing her moments with the kids somehow. Those moments with the twins had been precious but they had clearly come at a cost. Why could he not have his kids and his wife too?! Why was it one or the other? Why was she so distant from him, so cold?! Appearing like some kind of Stepford wife to the rest of the world, only allowing her flaws at home and even then, it was because he knew her, he knew what her flaws were, how she sank into her sadness. Or did he know her anymore? She hadn't touched him in years, she didn't talk to him anymore. They spoke and had conversations, but they never really *talked*. He knew she was depressed, had been for some time and couldn't understand why or what he could do to help, just watched on as the woman he loved seemed to slip away further each day. Despair gave way to feelings of anger. He *was* angry at her. Angry for leaving him because the Jenny he knew and loved wasn't there anymore.

Chris waited to see if Jenny would come down but it soon became clear she wasn't going to and so he resigned himself to another evening alone, flicking through the TV channels not really watching anything at all. Out of boredom he went to bed where Jenny lay awake listening to his movements, wishing for sleep to take her so she would be rid of the gremlin in her mind; the black cloud that swallowed her thoughts and poisoned them hovering over her.

As Chris slipped into bed, his aftershave triggered a wave of nostalgia. He had worn the same aftershave since they had met 12 years ago. Paco Rabanne Million. She had told him she liked the smell and he had worn it ever since. For her.

Jenny tried desperately not to cry, her throat aching with unshed tears while she waited for Chris to drift off to sleep. His breathing slowed finally, his body relaxing into the mattress more deeply; she could feel him as she stayed on her side of the bed, she knew him well. Relief that she could let go finally came when she crept stealthily downstairs after being sure Chris was asleep. She sat there quietly, the only sound the ticking of the clock as the thoughts ran round and round inside her mind. The blame that never went away, the guilt that tore at her insides, the constant feeling of failure of not keeping her babies safe was now combined with the torturous realisation she had kept their Father from them inadvertently by her own fear of not being good enough, taking over everything in her own mission to prove to herself and others she would do an amazing job at Motherhood. Seeing them tonight proved to her how wrong she had been, how many moments she had stolen and how happy they were together while she looked on in the side-lines; for those moments the roles had been reversed and Jenny couldn't stand it. It had hurt, like a physical wound in her chest; and yet Chris had suffered it for 5 years, never complaining just taking what he was offered and being grateful for that. Clearly loving them all with his great big heart, a love that she didn't deserve and couldn't reciprocate. Her own ability to give him affection crippled her heart. Jenny allowed the sobs to wrack her body silently, moving only to reach for the key to the liquor cabinet. She needed oblivion, no way would she sleep without it tonight and tomorrow they would have to build a snowman, so she had to be fresh.

The red liquid went down easily, slowly beginning to numb her senses, she started to feel it's effects after two glasses; three and she was woozy. Her mind still too busy though so a fourth was needed.

Jenny stared at their Christmas tree, their beautiful Christmas tree, decorated in the colours *she* chose, the way *she* chose. The colour theme running through the house on furniture *she* chose, placed where *she* chose. Jenny sank into herself once more. She had overshadowed Chris on everything, and he had simply loved her. The kids had been so happy for him to be a part of their special bedtime routine it was bittersweet to watch because they hadn't missed her. Not at all.

They don't need you. It was back again; those voiceless words jabbing her brain.

They don't need you. Jenny finished her glass and poured another.

They don't need you. It said over and over.

"You're right. They don't" Jenny finally conceded. She went to the medicine cupboard.

CHAPTER TWENTY-FIVE

"Jesus Jenny, what the fuck?!" Chris ran over to her slumped body reeking of red wine, the tablets spilled across her lap on the sofa.

"Jenny! Wake up! Wake up! How many have you taken?" Chris shook her violently, scared out of his wits. He never thought she would do this, they had problems, but it wasn't that bad was it?

"Jenny! How many have you taken?" Chris kept shaking her, trying to rouse her, terrified he was too late, groping round for his phone. He would call an ambulance that's what he would do. They would pump her stomach and it would all be ok.

"I didn't." She finally slurred.

Chris's eyes snapped back to her face, studying her. Was she lying?

"I didn't take any." Her heavy voice thick with alcohol insisted.

Chris exhaled; relief replaced with fresh worry "But you thought about it."

She couldn't look at him, she was still drunk, and things were hazy, Jenny thought it may even be a dream.

"Go away." She said.

"Go away? Yeah? Is that what you want? You'd like that wouldn't you." Chris spat at her. Anger replaced his concern seeing her so out of control. He didn't know what to feel right now. Was this how bad things had become? That she contemplated suicide? He looked around him, today was meant to be a special day, the beginning of Christmas, the first snow fall, and yet here was his wife creeping downstairs in the middle of the night to get comatose drunk and take tablets, so she didn't wake up again.

"How could you?" Chris looked at her accusingly "The kids they need you-how could you even think about it? I need you." He pleaded with her.

Jenny focused on him, things becoming a little clearer now.

"You don't need me." She said, "None of you do."

"Is that what you honestly think?!"

"It's true. You would be better off without me." She told him simply.

At least the alcohol had loosened her tongue for once and even if he didn't like it, he was getting to hear the truth of what she felt.

"Why? Because of one night I actually get to spend time with the kids. I read to them and tucked them in for a change? Is this why?!" Chris struggled to keep his voice down, he did not want the kids waking up and hearing this.

"No!" She laughed. "No." She shook her head vehemently, then lowered it. "Yes, sort of. I failed you Chris. I failed you all."

"How have you failed us?" Chris picked up her hand, wanting her to go on, needing to understand what had forever been left unsaid.

"I didn't do what I was meant to do. I didn't keep them safe."

"What are you talking about? You have always kept them safe Jen. You are the most careful parent I know; you would never put them in danger. Never."

"Not now, no. But before." She looked down and then laughed "You know those funny memes with the caption 'you had one job' That's me" She wasn't laughing anymore just staring down at her hands. "That's me."

"Jenny, I don't understand. You are an amazing Mum; you honestly are incredible. You put those kids above everything, every time."

She nodded and looked at him finally.

"And above you."

Her blatant truth stung him, bringing tears to his eyes.

"I know."

"I didn't mean to get between you and the kids but that's what I did, and I finally saw it. I saw it tonight. I have stolen so many things from you. So many things." Tears slowly rolled down her cheeks, she didn't attempt to wipe them away and Chris had no words. She had finally said what they both felt but he wasn't blameless; he had never wanted to upset her and had been walking on egg shells for as long as he could remember now, trying to appease her and bring her smile back to her face, that light laughter that lifted his heart when he heard it but it never came and things he had hated had become a way of life, without him rocking the boat.

"Jen, we both could have changed things-" He began.

"Don't make excuses for me." She insisted wiping her face with the back of her hand, shaking her head "I've failed you just as I have failed them."

"I don't understand how you have failed them." Chris couldn't understand.

"When they can't tie their shoes or say a word properly, make friends or don't understand something- It's because of me. My stupid weak body. I didn't keep them safe; it was my job to keep them safe and I didn't keep them safe."

"You think their early labour was your fault?!" Chris was just grasping what she said, "How could it possibly be your fault Jen?" He tried holding her and she pulled away.

"All I had to do was keep them safe and I couldn't even manage that. They weren't ready to be born Chris."

Realisation of the full extent of her guilt and needless blame that she had took on, hit Chris.

"Jenny," He said slowly, forcing her to look at him as he put his strong hands either side of her face, waiting until she brought her wet, sad eyes to his.

"That. Wasn't. Your. Fault." He said each word with the force he intended. She needed to know this.

"It wasn't." He repeated. "Twins are born prematurely all the time, and not just twins. It just happens. It's no-one's fault. No-ones" Chris spoke to her like he would a child, her tears flowing, sobs racking her slight body, making sounds he had never heard her make as her grief finally released itself.

"I'm sorry. I'm so sorry." She gasped between sobs.

"You don't have anything to be sorry about." He held her as she cried.

"For keeping you away. It's just-everything just-" She couldn't find the right words to express how she felt but Chris was beginning to get an idea of how big the weight she had been carrying around for so long actually was and he hated himself for not seeing it sooner. He had seen it but chose not to poke the fire while his polite, amenable wife had made life so easy; hating the way things had become over time.

"It hurts all the time." She finally managed.

"What hurts Jen?" Chris held her.

"Here." She sobbed holding her chest with one hand "And here." The other hand on her forehead. "I just want it to stop."

Chris cried along with her that night, for the years lost, the pain he could feel coming from his beautiful wife, the guilt he felt for letting her cover it up for so long and the relief that she had finally let it out, he held her, stroking her hair until she fell asleep on the sofa. Clearing away the mess of downstairs so the kids didn't see it when they awoke in the next few hours and settled down next to her, watching over her in case she woke.

CHAPTER TWENTY-SIX

Hayley loved Christmas, she loved the build-up, the decorations, the baileys! She even had special cinnamon spice candles for the evening making the place smell festive as well as looking it; the flat adorned throughout with Christmas decorations, little ornaments, Christmas globes, a moving Father Christmas, winter scenes with their own lights inside it sitting on the windowsill. Hayley stood back, surveying her hard work, very pleased with herself. The boys had had a lovely day helping out- well Sam did, Flynn took one look and disappeared into his bedroom shutting the door. It was always the same at Christmas and Hayley sighed, no matter how she tried to involve him she had come to accept that it wasn't Christmas he didn't like but the change in how things looked. It would take him a few days to get used to it then he would stare at the lights happily and laugh at the moving Father Christmas. Her and Sam had made paper snowflakes when they saw the snow start to fall and even better- settle! That could mean snowmen tomorrow or snow angels or snow ball fights! Hayley was excited, she really couldn't wait.

Watching it snow harder now outside as the boys slept soundly and she sipped her baileys, she sat back content.

Hayley's thoughts drifted to Simon and it irked her that she was still thinking about him. They had got on so well, the conversation never faltered, no awkward silences, it just flowed. She had felt happy being there with him and they had a lot in common too; not circumstances but music wise, the food they liked, how they loved the feeling of working out in the gym, same sense of humour too, Hayley remembered smiling. He had made her laugh and she him too, she acted the fool with him, and he didn't care, she was herself. It felt nice.

But Oh, who had time to arrange plans and then when they went awry because of the kids there was that stress on top of it as well; trying to balance everything just for an evening out. No, she shook her head, she could do without that stress thank you very much. Besides she just didn't trust men romantically and couldn't see that changing any time soon either. It was a shame though, she liked him a lot really, but men always wanted more didn't they.

Hayley watched the snowflakes fall, mesmerised by them and wondering if it was possible to just be friends with a guy.

CHAPTER TWENTY-SEVEN

Louise wrestled with the Christmas lights, cursing herself for not putting them away properly last year. I mean it only took five minutes, why couldn't she just do it and save herself this fight every time she hauled the Christmas boxes and the 8-year-old Christmas tree out of the loft.

The tree really needed replacing and every year for the past few years she had told herself she would get a new one, but it was nice once it was up, big branches that fanned out making it look bushy and full and with all the decorations on it and placed at the right angle you couldn't even see the branches that were missing. It was a good tree and had been there for all the girls Christmas's.

There was a box of all the little decorations that didn't match anything else, they were just fun to put on, a glittery penguin in a top hat, a toy soldier, a frog with a crown, music notes, all sorts of weird and wonderful items. Amy loved this part, she waited (almost) patiently for Louise to finish untangling the lights to wrap around the tree, playing with the shiny, glittery decorations in the box while Lucy looked up occasionally from the TV and then turned away again disinterested. She never got involved in this bit as much as Louise tried.

Once Louise was satisfied the lights were on the tree, she let Amy decorate. Amy spent ages choosing the different decorations, all different colours, shapes and sizes, painstakingly taking her time putting them just where she wanted them while Louise put some on the top half of the tree. Tinsel was draped over the TV, around the photos on the walls and in and out of the bannisters, little ornaments on the windowsill that she just knew the cats would swipe off at any given opportunity, the wreath on the door; it really was starting to look lovely. A little OTT her Mother would say (over the top) but that's what Christmas was all about.

After all the decorations had been put on just right, the tree turned to hide the missing branches and all dusty boxes back in the loft, Louise turned the lights off, leaving the Christmas tree lights on and they played their favourite game. Louise would tell Amy to find the Christmas frog and she would have to search for it on the tree, and the toy soldier, music notes, glass handbag, a pink bauble etc. Lucy played with the bottom baubles shining in the light.

They had chips on their laps for dinner, it wasn't healthy, but Louise hadn't felt like cooking after all that and now and again didn't hurt. It got dark quickly, the girls becoming sleepy soon after and it was only after putting them to bed she noticed the snow. Her heart leapt for a moment, oh how wonderful for it to snow on the day they put up their Christmas decorations! Louise turned around to share her joy and felt deflated realising no one was there; the kids were asleep.

Tomorrow would be fab if it settled, they could play in the garden, not for too long because Lucy hated it but Amy Oh, she loved the snow! Fingers crossed it would be there tomorrow. It hadn't snowed properly in years, she was so glad the girls were at home this weekend, even though she knew she shouldn't think it, but she wanted to see their little faces in the morning when they woke up to a blanket of snow and missing out on that would hurt. She wondered if Mark felt the same.

CHAPTER TWENTY-EIGHT

Jenny's head hurt. She had had hangovers before but this one was a killer. When she tried to move, pain splintered down one side of her head making her feel sick. Groaning, she tried to sit up then decided against it. Her eyes felt puffy and for a moment she was confused; hearing the kettle boil and Chris moving about in the kitchen, her cheeks reddened as she remembered.

Jenny peeked out of one eye, the light from the lamp immediately making her shut them tightly again.

"Here," Chris's voice was gruff, he sounded tired. "Take these." He handed her two paracetamols as she sat up, standing there with a glass of water. Her eyes adjusted and she took the tablets gratefully, seeing it was only 5:30. The twins wouldn't be up for a while yet, she had some time to get her act together.

Chris sat opposite her on the chair, his hands on his knees, leaning forward.

"We need to talk Jen. I know you feel like shit right now, but we need to talk at some point." Chris looked tired, like he hadn't slept at all. "Last night-"

"There's nothing to talk about." Jenny told him sharply "I was drunk. I was talking rubbish. Just forget about it. Forget everything I said."

"I'm not going to forget about it Jen. I think that's the first time you've actually been honest with me in years." Chris rubbed his temples. "I really think we need to talk to somebody."

Jenny's head shot up; she met his gaze "I'm fine Chris. Really. I just had a bad week and it all got on top. I don't know what I was saying. I'm going to have a shower before the kids get up. We're going to make a snowman." She smiled wanly. There was no emotion behind it and Chris felt defeated. Last night he had felt so close to her, hating the truth but feeling a connection with her at least and now she was backing away again; retreating into herself behind her invisible barrier. Polite and quiet.

Every step hurt her head, but she was determined to go and wash this feeling away, she wouldn't disappoint the kids. When they woke up, they would see the thick blanket of snow covering the garden and want to play in it. She could take some beautiful snow pictures of them all to go in the album.

An hour later, Jenny had washed and dried her hair, straightening the ends and carefully applied her make up. She needed extra concealer today and even though inside she wanted to throw up, on the outside she was definitely passable. Blue jeans, white rollneck jumper and a squirt of perfume, she was ready to make everybody breakfast and start the day.

Chris couldn't believe his eyes when she finally reappeared. How well she looked after last night and wondered how often she had been hiding those kinds of binges from him, he shook his head as she carried on like nothing had happened.

"Jenny-"

"I don't want to talk about it Chris. Ok?"

"No, not Ok. Not Ok. We need to talk."

He pulled her elbow until she turned to face him, and what he saw in her eyes scared him. She looked like a woman resigned to her sadness, not an ounce of fight left, just a shell; a shadow of who she used to be. Never fully loving or laughing anymore, just existing to carry out her duties.

This was not his wife. His passionate, exuberant, opinionated, funny, sarcastic wife who used to grab life by the balls. This was a sad woman who had given up. It made him angry, why wouldn't she fight for her family? For herself!

He let go with contempt; looking at her the way she felt to him, like a stranger.

The kids were up and by the sounds of it had seen the snow outside. They whooped and cheered, thundering down the stairs as fast as they could.

"Snow! Snow!" They both chanted jumping up and down still in their matching Christmas pyjamas.

"Yes snow! Shall we make a snowman today?" Jenny went to them, kissing them good morning.

"Snowman!" Paul agreed, grinning from ear to ear.

"And Daddy!" Mia joined in, clearly still happy about Chris being involved in their bedtime routine and wanting more of it today.

Chris said nothing, waiting to take Jenny's lead.

"Yes of course and Daddy too." Jenny smiled. Chris studied her, no hint of remorse or sadness there and wondered how she could hide it so well.

"I'll make us all breakfast first." Jenny told them and set to work in the kitchen, preparing their favourite pancakes and some for herself and Chris too, fresh coffee and orange juice. The table looked lovely when it was all set for them to sit down but Chris couldn't enjoy it; all those meals he had sat here marvelling at her cooking, the way she had a flair for setting the table, she had done it in hiding, hiding behind this fake-ness, lying to him, not really being there for him, not trusting him enough to share how she really felt. They used to be so close, why could she not share this.

Thoughts jumbled up inside Chris's head, over and over he went over last night, the things she had said, the pain he saw in her eyes. The truth she finally showed him and now she wanted to close up again. He was the closest he had been to her in years because he caught her binge drinking and close to taking tablets; thinking of ending her life, is that what it had to take?! Yet here she was now, morphing back in to the polite, perfect Stepford wife as if it hadn't happened.

Chris ate his pancakes, drank his coffee and joked with the kids. They didn't need to know anything and yes, they would all build a snowman and have a good morning, he would make sure of it.

The pure untouched snow was just waiting for them to dig their footprints in to it. Scrunching under their feet as they did so, the quietness in the air a quality that only snow could bring. Paul and Mia were thoroughly wrapped up in their coats. Hats, scarves and gloves waving their hands in excitement and literally jumping up and down. Chris showed them how to start off the snowman base with a ball of snow, compacting it then rolling it round the large garden until it became bigger and bigger. Jenny got a lovely photo of Chris, Paul and Mia pushing it round and round the garden; the snowman base getting bigger.

"Do you wanna build a snowman?" Chris had started singing.

"Yes!" Mia punched the air laughing.

The base done and Jenny made the head with the kids this time with Chris taking photos. If it hadn't been for last night this truly would have been the perfect morning. The pale sky and white background somehow made the world a quieter place, the only sounds to be heard were the kids laughing and Jenny's encouraging voice. He had to hand it to her, no matter how she was feeling she never let the kids down. Never.

The snowman head complete, all four of them heaved it on to the body, moulding it more with snow and patting it with their gloves to make it strong.

"Right kids, we need stones and twigs now." Chris instructed them and they set off about the garden trying to find stones under the snow, Jenny knew there would be some in the flowerpots so guided them over there but let them find them, Mia found the twigs and they began making the arms and mouth.

"Carrot now!" Paul announced. He ran inside, leaving footprints through the house on his way to the kitchen to find a carrot. Back two minutes later with their biggest carrot he pushed it in to the snowman's face, Mia made the snowman happy with the stones from the flowerpots, saving two of the biggest ones for his eyes.

"What shall we call him?" Jenny asked as they all stood back admiring their work.

"Happy." Mia said with a smile, clearly saying what she was feeling but it was a very fitting name for their snowman and so that's what they called it. Happy.

Jenny made them all kneel in front of Happy for a photo before the kids run off to play in the snow. They wanted to make snow angels. Both of them laid flat on the ground moving their legs back and forth over and over again, Mia lost her hat and so did Paul so when they stood up, it looked like the snow angels were wearing them. They giggled, wanting to leave them there so the snow angels didn't get cold. Jenny bundled them indoors, they were freezing and needed clean dry clothes on. She changed them and warmed them up with cuddles and blankets then made everybody some cheese on toast. It seemed like the perfect snack for today and put on Frozen 2 for the kids to watch while she cleaned the kitchen up. Chris was sitting with the kids watching the film, Paul on one side, Mia on the other all happy and content. If it hadn't been for last night and this morning, it would have been a wonderful weekend, If Jenny could have kept a lid on things. But she had had to go and ruin it hadn't she. Jenny noticed the hats beginning to get covered by fresh snow and thought she had better retrieve them before they were completely covered. Paul and Mia would need them in the morning for school. Jenny slipped on her boots and coat, stepping outside; the crisp air meeting her skin like a welcome burst of freshness. It certainly woke you up she thought as she crunched over to the hats picking them up. Jenny shook the snow off the lovely soft woollen hats, Mia had a pure white one and Paul loved red, so he had wanted a red hat. She remembered the day she had bought them; the kids were with her and they had run to them picking them out, Paul almost tripped over his own feet on the way back in his excitement to put it in the trolley and Jenny became so busy making sure he was ok, she didn't notice Mia wandering down another aisle looking for a matching scarf; In a split second she was gone. Jenny's throat was in her mouth, grabbing Paul she ran, leaving the trolley calling her name loudly over and over, the feeling of absolute dread overcoming her. It was less than a minute later she found her, but she would never forget that feeling, that feeling of utter panic of the fear of loss so great it was almost disabling. She didn't know what she would do without the kids, they were her reason for getting up in the morning, she simply would fail to exist she thought.

Chris left the kids curled up on the sofa, quite happy to watch the film quietly after this morning's fun in the snow, he was fading now and needed a coffee to keep him going after barely any sleep last night; switching on the kettle he noticed Jenny standing outside in the snow staring at the kids hats, completely motionless. He watched her for several minutes and she didn't move once. Fear enveloped him. What was going on with her? How quickly she could change from fun loving Mum to...what was this? She had promised him last night she would never think of doing anything like that again, she hadn't actually taken the tablets, but the intent had been there at some point. How long before she went a step further? Would he have to watch her every move from now on? She had refused to talk to him this morning, how could he ever help her if she wouldn't open up. Chris heard giggling from the other room, the twins laughing at something Olaf had done; they had seen the movie a dozen times, but they still loved it.

Anger began to bubble inside of Chris. Anger and resentment. She should be in here now enjoying this moment, getting warm, the four of them together on the sofa after a special morning of making the snowman. Or was that special? Was that an act like everything else, was she even in there anymore?

Jenny had been standing there staring at the hats for five minutes unaware of the time that had passed by, unaware of Chris who had stepped outside in his coat and boots, watching her watching the hats but not really seeing anything. Then it hit her, the hard snowball that broke up on impact, sending ice down her neck into her jumper. She dropped the hats; stunned. Her vacant eyes still not registering. The next one hit her in the chest. Jenny blinked, confused, looking up to see Chris scooping up more snow.

"What are you doing?" She asked him and tried to dodge the third that came flying her way. But Chris was a good aim and this one went in her hair. She shook it out, staring at him in disbelief.

"What are you doing Chris?"

"Fight back." He told her unsmiling. Then threw another, this landed under her neck, snow falling in chunks down her jumper, making her shiver.

"CHRIS!" She admonished him.

"Fight back." He growled launching another one, this time harder, hitting her in the face. "Fight back!"

Chris threw another and another and another, all landing on Jenny. The last one was hard and hit her in the eye. It hurt. A flash of anger ignited her eyes and she knelt down scooping up as much snow as she could, compacting it hard wanting to get him straight in the face with it.

"You bastard." She called him through gritted teeth and threw the snowball, Chris took it in the side of the head and carried on throwing snowballs at her as fast as he could, as hard as he could. Jenny was soaked now, her head throbbed, her hair stuck up, tears of confusion and anger stung her eyes, blobs of mascara had begun running down her cheek, she tried keeping up with his blows, but he was too quick.

"Fight back!" He told her over and over again, she ran over to him, pushing him over scooping the snow with her arm throwing it at him, he landed on his back, pulling her down with him, throwing her to the side. God he was strong! Jenny laid there a moment trying to catch her breath but wanting to retaliate as well, Chris rolled over on to his knees, he grabbed her coat with his fists, pulling her up to look at him "FIGHT BACK!"

Looking back at him he saw her, angry and fighting. Lost and desperate but still there; her once vacant eyes shining now with fresh emotion.

"I'm trying!" She shouted.

"I want my wife back." Chris whispered, letting go of her coat. Jenny fell back against the wet ground, soaking and dishevelled. "I want my wife back." He repeated, backing away from her, going back inside.

CHAPTER TWENTY-NINE

Louise rarely got excited about snow, but at the girls ages it was exciting, and they hadn't seen it for so long they had probably forgotten what it was like when it settled. She got up early to turn the Christmas lights on before they came downstairs, it always made her feel warm inside when the lights were on and still only beginning to get light outside; Christmas was a magical time. She put on the news quietly while sipping her coffee; it wasn't long before she heard the first signs of life from upstairs. Louise cocked her head to the side and listened. That was Amy, the footsteps were too quick to be Lucy. She heard her go and check in Louise's room first as she always did; when she didn't find her, Amy sat at the top of the stairs and bumped all the way down on her bum until she reached the bottom.

"Wow." She said in awe at the tree again as if she had forgotten what it had looked like from last night.

"Good morning beautiful." Louise grinned, making room for her on the sofa, but Amy stood in front of the tree taking it all in again for several seconds first before climbing up for a cuddle.

"Guess what?" Louise said teasingly.

"What?"

"It snowed last night." She told her happily.

Amy sucked in her breath dramatically then ran over to the front room window looking out at their now white front garden; all you could see was thick snow covering everything. Just the tops of bushes were visible, and it was still snowing. It was a blank canvas just waiting to be played in.

"Snow!" Amy literally shook at the sight of it, she ran to the porch grabbing her wellies and coat, still in her pyjamas and Louise laughed.

"You have to put gloves on Amy."

"Ok." She replied happily.

"Lucy isn't up yet babe, if you're going out there, go in the back garden. When she is up, we will make a snowman ok?"

"Ok." Amy wasn't listening, she just ran in to the back garden, marvelling at the beauty before her and began scooping it together making what would become the 'Snowblob' on the garden table.

Lucy got up soon after and wanted to join Amy, so before they had even got dressed and eaten all three of them made a snowman. Louise had to do it quick because Lucy would get so cold and literally turn blue in this temperature, but it was precious to watch them concentrating so hard on patting the snowman down, poking sticks into his sides and stealing Louise's hat to keep him warm. They didn't have a carrot so used a courgette instead. Amy looked at it questioningly until Louise told her that's what made their snowman unique, and they could name him Colin. It didn't last long all three of them in the garden, maybe 40 minutes or so but it was moments like this that Louise cherished, she took photos of the three of them still with bed hair and all in pyjamas, with Colin the snowman. She took photos of them smiling proudly at their creation and when they weren't looking. She never wanted to forget these moments and she was grateful to have them.

Amy insisted on staying outside for another half hour after Louise needed to take Lucy inside, she just loved the snow so much, but Lucy was too cold now, so Louise warmed her up inside while watching Amy, feeling very happy and lucky.

Later on that day Louise received a text from Mark.

Mark: Hi, did the girls build a snowman?

Louise stared at her phone; did he actually expect a response? The jerk! When she had asked him to text her when the girls were settled in bed the night they stayed over, he quipped 'If I get the time.' Arsehole. Yet, she kept looking at the question wondering how she would feel if it were the other way around. How would she feel if they were at Marks this weekend, seeing the first proper snowfall in years and not being able to share it with them? Despite their differences, they both wanted special moments and memories with the girls. Louise hesitated for a long minute then replied.

Louise: Hi, yes, they did. How about after they finish school tomorrow you come and build one with them out the front? Should still be snow for a couple of days.

Mark: Yes please! Thanks Lou.

He added a smiley face and although she would not be seeing them all day while they were at school, then going out to make a snowman with Mark meant they would be extra tired afterwards and only time for dinner and bed, she knew she had done the right thing. Mark needed his moments too. She just hoped he didn't bring what's-her-face. That would just be too much.

CHAPTER THIRTY

Hayley ducked as the snowball flew past her head.

"Ha! Missed!" Then launched one back at Sam, getting him on the shoulder. Sam packed up another snowball getting her this time as she ran away laughing. Flynn looked out every now and then, the look on his face showing that he really couldn't see why they wanted to be in the snow in the first place. He had point blank refused to go out in it, Hayley had anticipated this knowing what he was like with sandy beaches, and he really did hate the cold, so had invited her folks' round for a coffee, while they were there, she took the opportunity to play with Sam in the snow. This way everybody was happy, and she didn't feel guilty, well a little bit... she had barely said two words to her folks before grabbing her coat to run and play in the snow with Sam, but they would get over it. They understood.

"Take that!" Sam threw another, laughing as when Hayley tried to move out of the way, tripped over her own feet and landed face down in the snow.

An hour they played. The plan was to make a snowman, but they just had snowball fights instead. Wet through and shivering they went inside, their shoes making puddles on the wooden floor as they went.

Hayley dried off, put the kettle on for a cuppa and settled down to spin Flynn in his spinny chair, it was his favourite thing and would sit there for an hour while she would spin him round. OK, so he didn't join in, but he was happy doing his own thing, Sam got to play in the snow, so all in all a success, she even had a little chat with her parents before they went home.

It had been a nice day and Hayley was tidying up after the boy's baths and lighting her candles when she heard the buzzer go. She frowned, she never got uninvited guests, nowadays everybody texted first. It could be a cold caller and if it was, they would keep buzzing so she hurried to answer it before it woke the boys up.

"Hello?"

"Hi Hayley, It's Jenny."

Jenny? What on earth was she doing here? Hayley buzzed her in, opening the front door and waited while Jenny came through the landing. She had her head down, sniffing like she had a cold.

"Come in darling. Let's go straight through to the front room." Hayley didn't want to wake the boys; she could tell something was wrong.

It wasn't until she had closed the front room door, she noticed Jenny's appearance and was startled. Jenny looked a mess, her hair was fluffy and knotted on one side, her make up was halfway down her face although you could see she had tried to do something about it in the car, streaks of mascara were hard to get off and her eyes were all red and puffy, it looked like she had hurt her cheek too.

"Jesus Jenny! What happened to you?!" Hayley kept her voice quiet; she was shocked to see her like that and even more shocked when Jenny sat down on the sofa, putting her head into her hands beginning to cry. This was new. Jenny always came across as having everything together, something awful must have happened.

"What's wrong, has something happened? Are the twins ok?" Hayley sat next to her, putting her arm around her.

"The twins are fine. I'm sorry." Jenny managed to say through her tears "I -I didn't know where else to go."

"Well, whatever it is. I'm glad you came here. You look like you could do with a coffee."

Jenny looked up and nodded gratefully. This was not the person Hayley had met half a dozen times before, this broken, dishevelled woman was not the Jenny she knew. She went to make the coffee, fetching some tissues as well. Setting it down in front of her, Hayley took her own seat next to her again, concerned for her new friend.

"What's going on?" She asked gently.

"Chris and I had a fight." Jenny told her.

"Ok. What about? Must have been pretty bad to get you this upset."

"No. I mean an actual fight." She took a sip of the hot liquid; it burned her lips, but she was grateful for its warmth.

162

"A fight?"

Jenny nodded.

"You and Chris?" Hayley was gob smacked. They were not a couple you imagined having a fight. Not at all. Just earlier that day Hayley had seen the pictures on Facebook Jenny had uploaded, the family photos of their Christmas tree, the fireplace where they all stood, making the snowman, all together, like a happy family. Nothing looked out of place at all.

"Well, it was a snow fight...but...sounds ridiculous! Me and my husband had a snowball fight!" She began to laugh, a shrill, forced laughter that soon turned to sobs. Hayley took her coffee from her and held her while she let it out.

"I have really fucked up." Jenny breathed the words out through her tears.

Hayley stayed quiet, knowing Jenny needed to talk.

"I just feel so *empty* sometimes you know? And then I'm so emotional I can't think straight. Then there's days I don't feel anything and days where everything hurts and there's this thing on my chest that won't leave me alone. I feel guilty all the time and I feel sad. I feel really sad." She blurted it all out.

"How long have you been feeling like this?"

Jenny snorted a half laugh "Oh, I dunno. 5 years."

"5 years!" Hayley exclaimed.

Jenny nodded. "And It's just getting worse. It didn't start off this bad, it started off with the guilt and then everything else grew on top." Jenny sipped again at her coffee, gaining composure a little.

"Why do you feel guilty?" Hayley wanted to know, and Jenny was quiet for a while.

"You are a fantastic Mum do you know that?" Hayley told her firmly.

"No, I am not." Jenny seemed convinced of this. "I am not perfect."

"I didn't say you were perfect. None of us are perfect, and who would want to be?! What is perfect? A flawless individual with no personality, making everyone else feel inadequate? No thanks, give me a real person over that any day. Trying to be perfect is just setting yourself up for failure darling."

Jenny looked at Hayley, frowning as her words sunk in.

"Look I don't know what is going on, but I do know that you have a family that loves you, a husband who clearly worships you and they can't all be wrong can they."

"He didn't worship me today." Jenny looked down. "And I can't blame him."

"Does he know how you feel?"

"He does now, I think. I think I told him last night. I was drunk. I crept downstairs to drink while he was asleep, and he found me passed out with some tablets."

"Oh Babe." Hayley rested her hand on Jenny's shoulder.

"I didn't take any." She insisted "But it scared him, and me if I'm honest. I didn't realise I was getting that bad. It all came out, only because I'd been drinking though. I tried to forget about it today and carry on, but I couldn't, he won't let me. He's angry and scared and upset I didn't tell him."

She shook her head "We used to be so close, could share anything."

"So, what happened? Why can't you now?"

"I failed him and the kids and through my own fear of failing as a Mum I failed him even more. I've stolen moments from him that we should have shared, so many moments we will never get back because of my own hang ups. I realise that now." Her honesty surprised no-one more than Jenny herself, but she found no judgement here. Just compassion.

"Wow that's a lot of blame to carry Jen." Hayley sat back, she was a straight talker and that's just what Jenny needed right now. "Now I don't know what you are blaming yourself for, but I do know you haven't failed any of them, you are a great Mum and you always put the kids first. We all fail everyday though, I mean I swear when I shouldn't sometimes, I burn the dinner, miss appointments, I won't even go to those poxy school meetings anymore because they stress me out so I give them my input in different ways and let them all sit around the table discussing my son til the cows come home so I can crack on getting on with being his mum. Louise forgot to put knickers on Lucy last week! When the school rang her after P.E asking her about it, she was so embarrassed she blamed Lucy saying she must've taken them off herself!"

Despite herself Jenny laughed a little.

"But I do know one thing. You're down and you need some help and If you don't get it after knowing that, *then* you will be failing your kids. Because they need you Jenny and if you fall apart, they won't have you, will they?"

Jenny stared at Hayley; all her words made sense. She felt comforted too knowing Hayley didn't always do everything by the book and made mistakes too, maybe she had been too hard on herself over it.

"There's no shame in getting help Jen. I had to."

Now it was Jenny's turn to be shocked. This strong woman who shot from the hip, laughing and joking and bringing up two boys alone, and doing it very well as far as Jenny could see, who didn't need anyone, Louise's rock; *she* needed help.

"Yeah. When the boys were young. I had just had Sam; Tim had been gone a while and I was struggling. I denied it at first but in the end, I went to the doctor." Hayley frowned at the memory. "It was hard. It still is some days; but you know what I'm doing my best and that's all I can do and they" She nodded in the direction of where the boys would be sleeping "Know that 'cos they know I love 'em. *even* if I fuck up sometimes. It's ok to not be ok all the time, but you've got to let people help."

Jenny nodded, she felt like a little child learning to walk. She wasn't used to asking for help.

"But how do I do that?" She implored.

Hayley took her hand "Just ask."

CHAPTER THIRTY-ONE

It was past the kid's bedtime by the time Jenny walked through the door. She had just upped and left earlier, taking only her car keys and nothing else; driving round and round, not knowing where to go. She was glad she had gone to Hayley's, she needed someone to tell her what to do and Hayley was just the right person for the job. It dawned on her that tonight had truly cemented their friendship and she knew without requesting it that she wouldn't share it with anyone else; Hayley had needed help too at some point, she hadn't gone into detail but knowing that Hayley; strong independent Hayley needed to ask for help at some point gave her the courage to ask too. She just hoped her resolve wouldn't melt away as soon as she walked indoors.

Jenny closed the front door quietly behind her, Chris appearing almost instantly in the doorway of the living room, relief flooding through his face. He looked so worried. She hadn't even taken her phone; hadn't heard the missed calls and texts he had kept sending until he realised she had left it and stopped trying. She stood there for a moment, unable to look at him, not knowing what to say. His earlier anger still so fresh in her mind.

"I'm sorry." Chris began as he walked towards her. "I should never-"

"No, *I'm* sorry Chris. You've been nothing but patient with me." Jenny looked up, wondering what she had ever done to deserve such an understanding man, he who must love her so much was willing to forgive all her failings so easily.

"Up until now." He looked down, ashamed of himself. "I wanted to shake you. To wake you up, to snap you out of it. It was wrong."

"I don't think you were wrong. I think I needed it. You forced me to admit some things." She thought back to her earlier conversation with Hayley, grateful she was able to go to someone.

"What things?" Chris pushed.

"I need some help." She whispered. "I need your help."

Chris was over to her in two strides, enveloping her in his arms, tears choking them both as they held on to each other tighter than they ever had.

"I know." He kissed her hair, desperately relieved she had finally said it, finally admitted it. It wouldn't be easy he knew that, but he would be right there with her the whole time.

"We'll get through it together." He promised her.

The next day, Chris and Jenny both took Paul and Mia to school; Chris had decided to work from home. The ground was another blank canvas of snow, a fresh start. Yesterday's footprints gone. How beautiful, Jenny thought; wouldn't it be wonderful if every day was a blank canvas, a chance to retake the steps that had gone wrong before.

The kids loved both of them being there to take them, throwing snow at each other on the way. Jenny and Chris walked slowly behind, not talking at all but the feeling of togetherness was apparent and comforting. Jenny knew she wasn't alone in all of this anymore. It was nice just to walk quietly in the snow slowly behind the children knowing her husband was there. He knew the secrets she tried to chain inside her brain, and he loved her anyway, more than that he wanted to help her. Jenny knew she needed more than that and had agreed to speak to the doctor. It was the first step towards happier days Chris said, like the first step in the fresh clean snow she thought. In her mind in the side that crept up on her and tried to hold her under, would show her, her own footsteps walking alone on a path, before her footsteps faded beneath her; all around her until she was nothing, just disappearing into the air, evaporating.

But this path she was on now, the path she focused on today she had footsteps beside her, going at her pace; stopping when she stopped, moving when she moved but never leaving her side. Jenny chose this path; she chose Chris's help.

Jenny looked up at him and smiled, it was a sad smile but to Chris it was beautiful, because it was real and one day when she smiled at him, she wouldn't be sad anymore and until then he would simply be there holding her hand.

CHAPTER THIRTY-TWO

Louise watched through the front room window as Mark helped the girls make a solid round snowball, then showed them how to roll it around all of the garden until it got bigger and bigger, all three of them pushing it in the end; only stopping when they were satisfied with its size. He made a big deal of how to shape it and compact it, so it lasted longer before they started on the head. They could have gone to the park to do it, but Mark pointed out if it was in the garden, they would see the snowman they made every day until it melted away.

She watched them through the window sneakily, so they didn't see her, seeing him take selfies of the three of them in front of their finished snowman. The girls looked happy. It had been the first time they had played in the snow with their dad and Louise looked on fondly at them. It was nice to see. They were a family even if it was a little disjointed and she was glad she had made the offer; now she had taken that step perhaps Mark would be a little more amenable in the future with contacting her when the girls were staying with him.

The loud banging on the door told Louise the girls were ready to come in. Lucy didn't like to stay out too long anyway, and they had both been at school.

Opening the door, the girls red cheeked and happy; snow covering their warm moon boots, their matching pink gloves soaking wet.

"Come on in you two, let's get you warm." Louise ushered them inside, peeling off their gloves off and coats. Amy kicked off her boots sending snow flying everywhere and Lucy sat on the floor waiting to be helped.

"No-man." Lucy said, she had real trouble with her S's.

"Yes, you made a lovely snowman. I saw!"

Lucy grinned and crawled over to the sofa; she was really tired now.

"Thanks Lou." Mark said genuinely. "That was really special. Our first snowman."

She nodded, "Sure. I know how I would feel if I couldn't do those things with them."

"How did we get here?" He asked her, still longing for it to be fixed somehow.

"Please don't start." Louise stepped back, ready to shut the door.

"Look, I just mean- we could maybe do things better. For them."

"In what way Mark? Don't start trying to guilt trip me again. We didn't work out and as much as you say you love them; constant arguing in front of kids is not healthy. None of us were happy." Louise reminded him.

"I know that, I'm not saying that."

"So, what *are* you saying?"

Mark sighed "You don't have to do it all on your own. The appointments, play dates, school meetings. I want to help."

"You do?"

"Yes."

Louise sighed, he looked so genuine, so well meaning and he meant what he said- right now at this moment, until something came up. Something always came up. Their arrangement worked because it was easy- for him, so the girls didn't get let down.

"Give me a chance." He could read her and could see her reservations clearly "I will not let them down."

She nodded, seeing what it meant to him and knowing it would be good for the girls too, if he could only stick to his word.

"Every other Wednesday, the week you don't have them." Louise said, "Lucy has physio after school for an hour, you can take her and then pick Amy up afterwards."

"Oh." He looked taken aback "I've never taken her physio before." Seeing the look on Louise's face he quickly added "But I would love that, I want to be more involved Lou".

"Well let's just start with that." She said, not fully trusting it would happen and hesitant to let the girls know in case something came up. They needed their routine, especially Lucy who didn't cope very well with change so she would need to prepare her for it and if he cancelled...

"You've changed you know." He told her. "You used to be so easy going."

Louise rolled her eyes, could they not even have one conversation without any snide remarks between them. It was exhausting.

"Well, *I* became a parent Mark. Things change."

"If you had let me finish, I was going to say I know why, even if I was a bit slow on the uptake. They are great kids and you're doing an amazing job with them."

Now it was Louise's turn to be surprised, Mark never said anything nice to her.

"Thanks." She said a little awkwardly, she really wasn't used to getting compliments from Mark.

"Well, I'll see you all the weekend. Usual time, bye girls!" Amy ran over for a last hug and kiss, Lucy didn't get up, she was really tired, so he came in quickly to kiss her cheek then left.

Louise watched him go thinking maybe things could be easier between them, it would be better for everyone if they were. So hard to even remember back to a time when they were together and happy; but they were once. They had created these two incredible girls and for that she was forever grateful to him. He may have moved on, but she wasn't ready to yet, not because she still loved him, she didn't; there were days she barely tolerated him but because she just didn't know how to be in a relationship anymore *and* be the mum she needed to be for her kids, they were her all and every time she tried to date, more of her time got compromised, it became too planned for her. Chunks of her time not distributed as she felt it should be and the balance was never right, something always had to give and of course it would be the guy. She was ok with that. It might change in the future, but for now she was ok with that.

CHAPTER THIRTY-THREE

Turning her house keys over and over, Hayley sat in deep thought. She was in her gym gear, she really wanted to go; the boys were at school, her cleaning job had been cancelled again and it was Monday. She needed to exercise, to get rid of her excess energy, but it was Monday and Simon would be there. She wanted to see Simon, but what would she say? The way things had been left between them it was clear she would call, and she didn't. Would he even buy the whole "I put my jeans in the wash with your number in them" Line, even though it really wasn't a line, it was true. She wanted to see him though, but the whole idea of seeing him as a potential date just filled her with anxiety, no matter how much they hit it off. Maybe he wouldn't even be there she pondered and immediately dismissed it remembering him telling her it was the one day he could go during the day. Unless he didn't want to go in case he bumped into her. The rude cow that never bothered to text.

See! This is how stressful men are she told herself. Hayley sat there for a long moment.

"I want to go to the gym." She said out loud and stood up, walking out the door quickly before she could change her mind.

Hayley needn't have worried so much; when she arrived, she went to her favourite two machines, luckily, they were next to each other. The cross trainer and the rowing machine and started on the cross trainer, immediately popping her ipod on to listen to her playlist, glancing around surreptitiously to see who was about. The relief she felt was also tinged with disappointment but concentrating on her workout, Hayley soon got lost in her music and began enjoying the rhythmic movement, pushing herself to go further when her muscles started to ache. Sweat pouring from her, she took a break to have a drink, reaching down to grab her water bottle when she saw his feet. Simon's feet, she recognised the trainers. Slowly Hayley sat up, her heart beating double time now.

"Hi." She said a little uncertainly.

"Hi?" Simon made it sound more of a question. He looked just as good as the last time they had met, better probably because he hadn't started his workout yet and wasn't beetroot red in the face like she probably was right about now.

Hayley hated awkward silences and tended to talk fast and too much whenever that happened. It happened now.

"Look." She began, "I'm sorry I didn't call, but I lost your number. Well, I didn't lose it. I can tell you exactly where it is, but it fell to bits in the washing machine. Honestly." Simon opened his mouth to speak but she rushed on, "And to be honest even if I hadn't washed it, I'm not sure I would have used it. I mean I like you, we click and get on, but I don't date. It's that simple, I just don't date. I'm not ready for it. I'm tied to my sons, I can't make those type of romantic plans, my life is not simple like that. It's just not." Hayley looked away suddenly feeling embarrassed.

Simon smiled, "Look it's ok I get it. I'm not asking for you to change your plans for me and I'm guessing you don't get a lot of free time."

Hayley nodded, oh why was he so understanding? she was reminded again how nice he was, how genuine he seemed and began to feel a bit guilty for blowing him off before they had even begun. Habit probably, she told herself.

"So how about this? Come do weights with me."

"Weights?"

"Yeah, I need to rest in between reps, and you said you wanted to start doing them so at least we can have someone to talk to while we do them, it's better than doing them on your own."

Hayley had to agree. Weights sounded good, she nodded, smiling at him. It was strange how she liked his company so much, there was a definite attraction between them, but she couldn't take it further. Not now. Flirting was fun though and male company was nice. She consoled herself with the fact she had been upfront and honest with him, not leading him up the garden path and they spent the next couple of hours together lifting weights, talking in between and laughing. She would normally be too self-conscious to go and lift weights where all the beefy men liked to hang out but with Simon, she felt comfortable hanging out there and even got talking to a couple of the other guys too. When it was time to end her session, Hayley was sad to go, she had had a real nice time and there was no pressure attached to it at all. Simon didn't mention coffee for which she was glad, and she left feeling good.

"See you next week?" He asked as she left.

"Yeah, see you next week."

CHAPTER THIRTY-FOUR

It was the second week in December, the snow long since forgotten as the warmer sunny days that followed melted it too quickly, turning the roads to slush, mud being traipsed through the front door every time someone came home; but it had been nice while it lasted Jenny thought. The kids had loved playing in it, and they had even had a snow fight after school one day too. She smiled, it was far less forceful than the snow fight her and Chris had, much more fun too. The kids had laughed when Chris had slipped over on his back then decided to lay there making his own snow angel. It was a good memory and Jenny managed to catch it with a photo, then laid next to him to make her own snow angel, the coldness creeping into her neck making her wince in shock. Paul took a photo with her phone while she had her eyes closed, Chris looking at her and laughing. She didn't even realise until later on when she was looking through them that it had been taken. Her hand hovered over the delete button then she saw Chris's face; it was pure joy looking at her. His eyes all crinkled around the edges. Clearly loving the sight of Jenny on her back in the snow. It wasn't picture perfect, *she* definitely wasn't picture perfect, her eyes screwed up, her mouth sucking in the cold air in surprise as the cold hit her neck, but it was a good photo and it made her smile remembering the day, that moment, the kid's laughter. She kept it.

Jenny had been to see the doctor. Chris came with her. At first Jenny found it hard to speak but Chris held her hand, squeezing it gently; silently reminding her he was there for her and slowly she spoke. The words unwilling at first, not making a lot of sense, jumbled together, hindered by her tears. Tears that were once held back so fiercely, but now came so readily at all kinds of inconvenient times. Chris told her it was good, she needed to let her emotions out and not coop them up inside anymore. Jenny felt like she had already cried a river, after each purge she thought there couldn't possibly be anything left, but there always was.

The doctor referred Jenny to a councillor and prescribed her some tablets, holding her hand up at Jenny's immediate protest.

"Just try them for a couple of weeks, they may help take the edge off. I've only prescribed a low dose and If you feel they are not working for you then stop taking them and come back to see me. They are not a long-term solution."

Reluctantly Jenny took the prescription, she didn't like taking tablets, then laughed at the irony of her thoughts when the image of her drunkenly slumped on the sofa with the bottle of paracetamol flashed before her mind.

If these helped her to stop getting to that point, then she will at least give them a go.

It had been ten days now and she was feeling more levelled out than she had in a long time. Not Ok. But the constant ups and downs of her emotions were far less violent than they were before. She just wished she could stop crying.

She had been avoiding Hayley's texts mostly. Hayley didn't want to bombard her, but she wanted to know if she was doing ok to which Jenny replied,

"Yes, I'm ok. Thank you for the other night." With two kisses when Jenny would normally only put one, so she would know she wasn't being funny, she just didn't want to talk. Hayley respected that, she knew what that felt like and gave her space only texting every few days to let her know she was there if she needed to talk or simply say hello. It was comforting, Jenny had never had a friend like that before, someone who had seen her so low and been there to help, to offer a friendly ear and some straight-talking practical advice. No judgement at all. Jenny was scared of judgement from people, when the only people that really mattered were right here in this house with her. She didn't know why or where it came from, but it started when Paul and Mia were born and had grown bigger with time along with her fear of failure. It was probably connected but she decided not to think about it right now as Chris brought her some lunch. He had been cooking a lot more lately and he was a good cook! She had forgotten how good he was, preferring the more kid friendly meals to the spicy concoctions he used to knock up for her, remembering the flavours when she tasted it. Memories of him cooking for her, and she for him came creeping back to her as they shared their lunch while Paul and Mia were at school.

Chris had been working from home a lot more lately; Jenny knew he was still worried about her, but she liked having him around instead of being left alone with her thoughts.

"Oh, this is gorgeous!" She exclaimed. "Probably too hot for the kids though."

"Well, we can always try them and see, you never know Jen."

She nodded; she was so used to choosing everything it was hard to step back a little. But she had to try.

School runs were different. Chris wanted to come along each day, which the kids loved. Jenny came to realise it wasn't Daddy they preferred, but the two of them together. Their faces lit up when they came out of school seeing them both standing there waiting for them, ready for a hug and questions about their day. They seemed happier.

A little red headed boy began to join them after school, chatting away a mile a minute while Paul and Mia smiled and nodded, not able to keep up with his constant chatty flow but happy to have made a friend, they would walk all the way to the main road past the large field together where Robert would turn left, and they would turn right.

"He just never stops talking!" Robert's mum exasperated with a smile one pick up time while they walked along behind the kids watching them share a bag of sweets.

"I'm Sarah by the way." Robert's mum offered.

"I'm Jenny, this is my husband Chris."

"Nice to meet you. The twins are all Robert talks about; he just loves them!"

"Oh, that's so nice," Jenny said. "Is he new here?"

"New? No. Robert and your two have been friends since September, but I had to pick him up ten minutes early for a while, so we didn't really get to see you after school. My eldest daughter is at secondary and settling in, both finishing at the same time, teething problems at the school..." She sighed. "Never ending is it? If it's not one thing to worry about it's another. But she is more confident getting the bus now so hopefully it will work out better and not such a mad rush all the time."

Jenny was stunned into silence, she thought the kids didn't have any friends at school, they had mentioned a Robert now she thought about it, but she thought it was from a PE game or something. After hearing that woman's comment at the gates before Jenny had developed a mistrust and low expectations of people, she had been wrong, she realised as she watched Robert genuinely enjoying his time with Paul and Mia and even practicing his signing with them too. She had judged too quickly, had done what she feared others would do.

"Robert is getting good at some of the signs, has even taught me a few as well." Sarah told her. "The teacher is doing it more in class and a lot of the kids are picking up. I think it's great, they should teach it as a lesson."

"Wow I didn't realise." Jenny thought of Mrs Mally and the hard time she normally gave her, making her think maybe she needed to give people more of a chance. She was glad she had met Robert's mum. Knowing they had a friend at school made Jenny realise it wasn't them against the world, she just had to open herself up to trust people more then she would see the good in people and not the bad. As they all waved goodbye, Jenny saw the kid's happy faces, their hands in hers and Chris's. Why hadn't she seen this before? Maybe she just couldn't because she was so low, fighting all the demons in her own head. Yes, there were people that didn't understand the twins needs and there probably always would be but there were also people that maybe didn't understand but tried to and accepted them as they were. Jenny always got out of the school grounds so quickly to avoid overhearing any more hurtful comments she hadn't spent the time to look around and see the people that were decent and nice. She hadn't realised how closed her eyes had been until Chris had helped her to open them... With a snowball.

The next text that came through was hard to ignore. It was Louise arranging a Christmas playdate for the kids. That was something she would always do. Paul and Mia loved being with their friends and had picked out presents for them, painstakingly wrapping them and signing their name on the Christmas cards. It would be nice, Jenny was anxious though, she hadn't seen Hayley since that night she turned up at her house a real mess, but she couldn't say no to the kids. Louise had suggested wreath making at her house, play centres would be too busy where it was so cold; all the families were doing indoor activities now and Lucy was only good for a little while outdoors. There were reindeer at the garden centres, but the queues would be so long, none of the kids were very good at waiting in line, it was stressful to even think about it.

Wreath making, hot chocolate and a Christmas film was on the agenda instead, Louise made it clear not to worry how long the kids lasted. She knew from experience that playdates could last for three hours or fifteen minutes depending on how they were all getting along. Jenny relaxed a little, they really got it these two she thought, they really did.

Saturday morning, Jenny made sure she had snacks, the Christmas cards for Hayley and Louise and all the kids, a separate one for each; Paul and Mia had loved writing out their friends' names with help from Jenny and Chris. She had flowers for both Hayley and Louise and a bottle of wine each too, the kids all had a gift, nicely wrapped in red with a gold bow on top. She loved wrapping presents, it really was feeling Christmassy now and Paul and Mia were getting more excited each day when they opened another door on the advent calendar.

They pulled up at Louise's, Paul and Mia desperate to see their friends, each holding a bag of presents and cards to give out once they got there. Jenny hadn't been to Louise's before and needed the sat nav to help her find it. Once she got to where the satnav took her, she found herself in a large carpark, not knowing where to go. There was a long path with houses on the left, maybe it was down there. They made their way down, looking for the right number.

"10!" Paul shouted when he spotted it first, running towards the door with Mia following closely behind.

Louise opened the door wide, a big grin on her face.

"Hi!" She stepped aside for her guests to come inside "Come in! Wow, don't you two look gorgeous." She said to Paul and Mia. They really did, both in blue jeans and warm boots, Mia wore a yellow rollneck under her white coat and Paul wore a white one under his black coat. Amy greeted them as soon as they walked in, helping them take their coats off and showing them where to kick their boots off while Lucy slowly made her way over to Jenny. She didn't always go straight to other children, preferring the attention of adults; Jenny bent down for a hug with Lucy before accepting Louise's hug hello.

"Oh, your house looks so festive! I love it, Your tree too. It's beautiful! Is that a frog?" Jenny asked on closer inspection.

Louise nodded solemnly "A royal frog."

"Oh, I stand corrected. Of course, It's a royal frog." Jenny laughed, glad she had come, feeling much more at ease already.

Amy had taken Paul and Mia over to her dolls house to show them all her little dolls and furniture, they were all playing with it, organising the rooms when Hayley arrived.

Amy squealed knowing more of her friends had arrived and Paul and Mia looked up expectantly. Jenny suddenly felt anxious wondering how Hayley would be with her after that night, but she didn't have much time to worry about it too much as chaos ensued immediately after. Flynn was upset and moaning, seeming not to want to be there at all and Sam ran straight over to the others to play while Lucy tried to grab Flynn to help calm him down. Hayley was red in the face as she battled to keep Flynn from kicking at the front door and Louise ran upstairs saying something about the DVD player.

Jenny didn't know how to help, feeling useless she simply stood there for a moment then decided to take Lucy to the sofa, she knew Lucy wanted to help but right now they needed space. Then Louise came downstairs taking two at a time.

"DVD player is on in my room." She told a relieved looking Hayley.

"DVD Flynn?" That caught his attention. "Upstairs?" Hayley's voice sang, a little strained.

Flynn spun round on his bum and shuffled over to the steps, crawling up them seeming to know where to go.

"Thanks babe." Hayley told Louise "What did you put on?"

"Alvin and the chipmunks."

"Great." She said in a sigh. "What a morning!" Hayley finally took her own shoes off and coat, turning to kiss them both on the cheek.

"Cor It's a dry house in here!"

Louise rolled her eyes. "You have literally just walked through the door. Hang on I'll put the kettle on princess."

Jenny smiled; they were at it again. Coffee sounded good. Louise pottered about in her small kitchen making coffee, she had laid out all the things they needed for the wreaths on the table; polystyrene circular ring, pinecones, glue with 6 separate tubs, paint, plastic holly, glitter, old baubles and little bits of Christmas decorations.

"Wow you are prepared Louise." Jenny remarked, "I could have brought something with me." She felt bad Louise had gone to all this trouble and they hadn't contributed.

"Oh, that's ok it was really only the rings and holly I had to get, the rest I had anyway."

"Glitter!" Hayley laughed "Are you mad?"

"It's an old carpet." Louise said dismissively.

"Rather you than me babe." Hayley sat down with her coffee, along with Jenny and Louise as they watched the kids play around the base of the Christmas tree, ignoring the wreaths, content to be with each other making up a game with all the characters from the doll's house. Amy had brought down her farm animals, she had hundreds of them, she loved to role play with them and the four of them were immersed with the game. Lucy had crept upstairs to sit with Flynn who refused to come down again and the three women ended up making the wreaths themselves. Jenny noticed how competitive the two friends were with their wreaths, trying to make their one better than the other. They were like big kids, but it was fun, even if the kids weren't interested.

Talk turned to their week and Louise told them about her conversation with Mark.

"I think we've kind of turned a corner." She told them. "I hope so anyway, it's not a nice way to have to be every time we see each other."

Hayley nodded, "That's good babe, I just hope he sticks to his word for them."

"I hope so too, I have to give him the chance to don't I." Louise cleared away the wreaths to make room for the snacks instead, putting a Christmas film on.

"Who wants hot chocolate?!" She asked them.

"Me!" Came the resounding reply of the four of them still playing under the tree, now adding a Lego creation next to the doll's house with different levels; it was a hospital Paul informed Louise.

Louise made hot chocolate for the four of them, she encouraged Flynn and Lucy to come down, but they wouldn't budge.

"Leave them babe, they prefer it quieter anyway." Hayley reminded her. "I do wish he would join in but It's just not his thing and when I make him, I'm doing that for me and not him, I've realised that. He is happy where he is, Lucy too right now so don't worry mate." When she saw Louise's face of disappointment coming downstairs again without them.

"Well, it's just hot chocolate for us now then." She went into the kitchen to warm the milk.

"Did I tell you about my new gym buddy?" Hayley began.

"No." Louise called from the kitchen "What's she like?"

"Well, *he* is actually a good crack, helps me with my reps and we do our weights together on a Monday." She hid her smile behind her hand as Louise came out of the kitchen, eyebrows raised.

"HE?"

Jenny leaned forward; her chin rested on her hands "Tell us more." She encouraged.

"Well, It's just a friendship-"

"Ha!" Louise stopped her "They don't exist between males and females." She lowered her voice so the kids wouldn't hear "Guaranteed. One of you wants to bone the other."

Jenny snickered at Louise's choice of words, checking the kids weren't listening.

"No-one is boning anyone." Hayley told her "Just friendship honest. I was straight with him, told him I don't do dating and I don't want to, or have time for it."

"Really?" Louise sat down surprised.

"Yeah" Hayley smiled, remembering "And he just said ok, let's do weights so we've been meeting on a Monday and we do weights together."

"Smart guy." Louise concluded "He's playing the long game. He must really like you."

"Well maybe he is." Hayley confessed. The idea hadn't been lost on her either, also filling her with a kind of lift of the possibility of it. But she had been straight with him and he still wanted to spend time with her, she liked him even more for that. "And if he is, maybe you never know."

"Well, if he does decide to wait, you're worth waiting for." Jenny told her.

Hayley smiled, tears welled up in her eyes, she felt so lucky to have friends like these.

"Ah! Enough of all this lovey dovey stuff" She cried, "Where's this hot chocolate?"

"It's coming!" Louise carried out three steaming mugs of hot chocolate, she had added marshmallows on top with grated chocolate "There's a little something extra in there too." She winked.

"Baileys?" Hayley knew her friend so well.

"Just a little." She smiled.

"So, Jen. I went on Facebook earlier and I saw a photo of you in the snow with Chris." Hayley threw the comment at Jenny and she reddened immediately. Louise had seen it too; it was so different from what she would normally post. It was a great photo, but it wasn't exactly flattering, although it really had made her smile; it looked like a real fun photo.

"Bit different." Hayley pushed with a smile in her voice, Jenny would have to get used to Hayley's sense of humour and her tact or sometimes lack of it, but she knew when the time to be tactful was.

"Ah that." Jenny laughed, it had taken a lot for her to post that photo, she normally would only post pictures that were perfect, hair and make up done just right, all smiling at the camera, posing, clothes tidy etc but this was nothing of the sort at all; yet whenever Jenny looked at it she saw Chris's face looking at her with love in his eyes and could still hear the kids laughter that warmed her heart.

"Well, I'm not perfect." She told them with a smile.

"I will drink to that" Hayley met her eyes in a silent understanding, holding her mug up.

"Me too!" Louise joined in holding her hot chocolate mug up in the air.

"Me too." Jenny said.

The three of them chinked their mugs together, marshmallows sticking to their upper lip. Jenny watched as her kids played happily, listened as Hayley and Louise bickered good naturedly and she felt good. She felt real, she didn't need to pretend; not with these two anyway. Their honest nature and brutal but caring truth with each other had shocked Jenny at first, now she saw it for what it was, friendship. True friendship and jenny felt she belonged. She was far from ok most days, but she was learning that was ok; she would get there eventually, so long as she didn't carry that burden alone anymore and sitting here amongst true friends, the way Chris had stood by her, she knew she didn't have to.

The end

Printed in Great Britain
by Amazon